THE 'ANTELOPE' COMPANY ASHORE

The *Antelope* Company Ashore

WILLIS HALL

THE BODLEY HEAD

LONDON

British Library Cataloguing
in Publication Data
Hall, Willis
The Antelope company ashore.
I. Title
823′.914 [J] PZ7
ISBN 0-370-30775-5

© Willis Hall Productions Ltd 1986
Phototypeset by Falcon Graphic Art Ltd
Wallington, Surrey
Printed in Finland for
The Bodley Head Ltd
30 Bedford Square, London WC1B 3RP
by Werner Söderström Oy
First published 1986

1

Millie put the plateful of jam tarts carefully in the very centre of the table and then stepped back to admire the overall effect.

"Well now!" she murmured to herself. "That's what I calls a birthday spread an' a n'arf is that! Enough to feed a regiment of troops!"

And had there been anyone else in the dining room, there could have been no argument with the housemaid's statement.

It *was* a birthday spread and a half!

There *was* enough to feed a regiment of troops—well, almost.

There were three kinds of sandwiches; there were fruit tarts; there were currant tea-cakes, buttered scones, butterfly buns, maids-of-honour, seed cake, sponge cake filled with home-made raspberry jam, trembling transparent jellies, a towering milky-pink blancmange—and a score of other things besides.

Cook had certainly surpassed herself.

Millie rubbed her hands together in anticipation of the joyful afternoon to come and scurried from the room. As she crossed the landing she could not resist a peep into the parlour through the partly open door.

The room had been cleared of all its furniture, apart from

the piano, to make room for the rows of chairs which had been hired especially for the occasion. Coloured paper-chains hung from the ceiling. The walls were festooned with balloons of all colours, shapes and sizes.

Millie poked her head a little further round the door in order to get a better look.

"Did you require me, Millie?"

Millie jumped in startled surprise.

Mr Garstanton, her employer, was standing at the very back of the parlour setting up his bulky camera on its tripod.

"Lor', sir! No, sir! You did give me a shock! I was just admiring all the trimmings. Are you a-going to take a portrait of the parlour, sir?"

The year was 1899 and Ralph Garstanton was a professional photographer well known in the town. He had, during a long and illustrious career, photographed many civic dignitaries: any number of councillors, several aldermen and, on one never-to-be-forgotten occasion, a real lord mayor.

"Not a portrait of the *room*, Millie," said Mr Garstanton. "But I intend to take some photographic studies of this afternoon's festivities. After all, it isn't every day one has a genuine oriental conjuror in one's home."

"It ain't, is it, sir?" said Millie with an excited shiver. "Just think of it, eh? A proper real live Chinaman in this very room doing magic tricks! I'm that looking forward to it! I en'arf glad I came to work 'ere! It's one birthday party after another in this 'ouse, I swear it is! First Master Gerald's eleventh; now Miss Philippa being ten. Lawks-a-mercy! I'm ever so excited! I reckons I'm in as much of a tizzy as Miss Philippa is 'erself!"

2

With which announcement Millie, who seemed to do everything at the double, sprinted from the room.

Mr Garstanton smiled to himself and went on setting up his camera.

Gerald and Philippa Garstanton were the old photographer's grandchildren. Their father, who was a captain in Queen Victoria's army, was off on a tour of duty in India and their mother had gone with him. While their parents were abroad, the children were living with their grandfather in his house above the photographic studio. Mr Garstanton did his very best to keep his grandchildren happy—to which end he had hired the Chinese magician to come and entertain at Philippa's birthday party.

"Imagine, eh?" chuckled Grandfather Garstanton to himself, "a real Chinese magician!" And he too rubbed his hands together in pleasurable anticipation, just as Millie had done.

But if the Chinese conjuror filled the thoughts of both the photographer and the housemaid, the children themselves had other problems on their minds at that particular moment.

Gerald and Philippa, in the big nursery on the floor above, were both kneeling on the fireside rug and peering in through the windows of the tall dolls' house.

"They're not *still* sulking, are they?" asked Philippa.

"They jolly well are!" replied her brother.

"Open it up and let's *talk* to them," said Philippa.

But as Gerald moved to lift the catch on the front wall of the dolls' house, the door to the nursery burst open and Millie bustled in. Gerald gulped and took his hand away from the dolls' house. Philippa held her breath. They both stared up at the housemaid guiltily.

3

"You pair do well to look at me like that!" said Millie. "Haven't neither of you even *started* getting ready yet?"

Gerald and Philippa sighed with relief. Their well-kept secret had remained undiscovered yet again.

"Not yet, Millie," said Gerald. "There's ages to go before the party."

"Ages and ages," added Philippa. "It was clearly printed on the invitations—it doesn't start until three o'clock."

"Hoity-toity!" sniffed Millie. "All of an hour away at least. If it was *my* birthday party, I'd 'ave been straight into my party frock the minute my 'ead was off the pillow this morning—if I'd ever 'ad a party frock, which I've never." But Millie could not remain out of temper with the children for long. " 'Ere—innit a lark, eh?" she continued, her voice rising with excitement. "Innit a regular scream! A Chinese conjuror, no less! You'd better start getting ready soon! I'm off to see 'ow Cook's getting on with them curd tarts in the kitchen!"

Once again, Millie was off and out of the room in double-quick time.

The children exchanged a smile and then returned to the serious business in hand. Gerald opened the front of the dolls' house.

Inside the dolls' house was the *big secret*.

Three little people, none of them taller than fifteen centimetres, stood on the ground floor of the dolls' house looking up at the children crossly.

Spelbush, Fistram and Brelca were the only survivors of the shipwrecked *Antelope*. The *Antelope* was a ship which had sailed across eight oceans all the way to England from Lilliput some months before.

Gerald and Philippa had discovered the three tiny shipwrecked mariners at the seaside and had brought them home. The Lilliputians, on their part, had agreed to throw in their lot with the children rather than allow themselves to fall into the hands of any giant grown-ups.

The children had managed to keep and feed and clothe the little people all this while without their grandfather or Millie or the cook discovering they were there.

In fact, only two other people knew of the existence of the Lilliputians. Their names were Harwell and Sarah Mincing. They were brother and sister and they had been trying to get their hands on the little people in order to line their own pockets.

"Spelbush? Fistram?" said Gerald, pleading with the two small sailormen.

"Brelca?" added Philippa, addressing the lady Lilliputian.

But the three had decided they were still not speaking to the Garstanton children.

"Have you ever noticed, Fistram," said Brelca, ignoring Philippa, "that there's the most dreadful draught in this dolls' house—particularly when some bad-mannered, uncaring person opens the *entire* front wall?"

"It's my opinion," replied Fistram, who was tall (for a Lilliputian, that is!) and thin and forever eating, "that it's high time we found ourselves somewhere else to live."

"We might consider moving out of this district altogether," suggested Spelbush, who was short and round and considered himself the leader of the shipwrecked sailors.

"What a perfectly ideal solution!" cried Brelca, gleefully clapping her hands. "Personally, I've never really liked it here. I don't care for the view. Who wants to live in a dolls'

5

house that looks out directly over a coal scuttle? It's very common!"

"Stop it, all three of you!" snapped Philippa, almost losing her temper. "Stop it this minute!" There were times when she felt that their three visitors were not grateful for a single thing the children did for them.

"We *can't* take you downstairs to the party with us," said Gerald, mentioning at last the real reason why the little people were not speaking to them.

"We're only thinking of *your* safety," Philippa pointed out. "It would be far too dangerous for you on the parlour floor—there are some *very* clumsy children coming. You might easily get trodden on during Blind Man's Bluff."

But the Lilliputians were still not satisfied.

"You could take us down and hide us somewhere before it all began," said Spelbush.

"We could stay hidden all afternoon and watch the fun," said Fistram.

"Under the sofa," said Brelca.

"Behind an ornament on top of the whatnot," said Spelbush.

"In the sideboard cupboard with the door ajar," said Fistram.

"And have someone come across you during Hunt-the-Thimble?" said Philippa. "Then there really would be trouble!"

"We'll tell you all about it when everybody's gone," said Gerald.

"And we'll smuggle you up some food," offered Philippa.

"Madeira cake?" asked Fistram. "And pink blanc-

mange?" Fistram was particularly fond of pink blancmange.

The children nodded eagerly.

"There's sherry trifle too," said Philippa. "It's got real
sherry in it. I watched Cook pour it in."

"Perhaps they *are* right, you know," said Fistram to his
companions. "It would be rather dangerous down there—
think of all those *feet!*"

"You don't care about anything, so long as your stomach
is taken care of," replied Spelbush. "*I* wanted to see the
Chinese magician."

"He isn't a *real* magician, Spelbush," said Gerald.

"Not real?" asked Brelca, puzzled.

"No, of course he isn't real," said Philippa. "They're
only conjuring tricks he does. It's just pretend magic."

"Just pretend!" Brelca was outraged. "I'm sorry, little
girl, but wild horses wouldn't drag me to your birthday
party. I never attend functions that aren't genuine. Who
cares about a children's birthday party anyway? It's hardly
the social event of the season! You wouldn't catch me dead
at it—I'm much too grand for parlour games."

"Madeira cake, pink blancmange and sherry trifle,"
listed Fistram who, as Spelbush had rightly pointed out,
was only concerned with food. "What about a sausage-roll
as well?"

"We promise to bring you a sausage-roll," said Gerald,
solemnly. "If there are any."

"It's a bargain, then," said Fistram. "We'll stay up here
in the nursery."

Which seemed to resolve the situation happily for all
concerned. Gerald and Philippa, relieved, began to get
ready for the party.

7

"I hope there *are* sausage-rolls," said Fistram. "I do enjoy a nice sausage-roll."

In fact, there were to be sausage-rolls in plenty. Cook had just taken a whole trayful out of the oven. Millie had just burnt her fingers trying to filch one.

"Ooooh!" said Millie, blowing on her fingers.

"Serves you right, my girl!" said Cook. "You can just leave them alone—they're spoken for. I've a lot of hungry mouths to feed this afternoon."

" 'Ere!" said Millie, running her forefinger around the top of a cream bowl instead. "What about this Chinese conjuror, Cook? Will 'e be sitting down to 'is tea with the rest of 'em?"

" 'Course he won't!" said Cook. "The very idea! Chinese conjurors aren't *guests*, you silly girl!"

"Aren't they, Cook?"

"I should hope not! They're tradesmen, aren't they?"

"Don't ask me," said Millie, licking the cream off her finger. "I've never ever see'd a Chinese conjuror—I saw an Irish chimbley-sweep once."

"Oh, yes—they're tradesmen right enough is Chinese conjurors," continued Cook. "If he wants a bite of Christian tea, this oriental chap, he'll be having it down here."

Millie's eyes widened. "With us?" she gasped. "In this very kitchen?"

"That's right. Where else?"

"Lor' luv-a-duck!" said Millie. "What, sitting down at this very table, as large as life an' twice as natural?"

"Of course."

"I say, eh? I wonder what'll take 'is fancy? Do you think they eat sausage-rolls then, Chinese conjurors?"

" 'Course they don't!" Cook snorted. "Didn't they learn

you anything at that orphanage? They eat rice-pudding, don't they?"

"Rice-pudding?" asked Millie, wide-eyed with astonishment.

"That's it—rice-pud."

"Nothing else?"

"Not as far as I've been led to believe," said Cook.

"Yerks!" said Millie, pulling a face.

"It's what they've been brought up to," said Cook. "They *like* it. Besides, it wouldn't do if we was all to eat the same things, would it now? Roast joints of beef and best boiled ham and that. There wouldn't be enough of that to go round everybody in the world." Cook glanced up at the ceiling and lowered her voice as if she was in church. "So, in His infinite wisdom, the good Lord made it so's we all eat different. And the Chinese got rice-pudding."

"Well, I never!" exclaimed Millie.

"I've got some in the larder for him," said Cook. "It's cold from yesterday, if he fancies it."

"Cor! Fancy being alone in a room with a Chinese conjuror, eh?" said Millie, her eyes darting nervously around the kitchen. "The very thought of it makes me go all goose-bumpy!"

Harwell Mincing, the out-of-work fairground showman, examined his latest disguise in the long mirror in the living room of the lodgings he shared with his sister, and a slow smile spread across his face. The smile hovered uncertainly for several seconds, surprised at finding itself in such an unusual spot—it was not often that Harwell Mincing smiled. But, on this occasion, Harwell was well satisfied with what he saw.

9

He admired the long drooping oriental false moustache that hung down from either side of his upper lip. He admired the oriental, finely worked brocade hat perched on his head. He admired, too, the long colourful oriental brocade gown he was wearing that reached down to the floor.

Harwell practised a few oriental gestures in front of the mirror with his hands.

"And who do we think we are today, brother, might I ask?" snapped a voice at his back. Harwell's sister, Sarah, had come into the room.

Sarah Mincing, who was as mean and hard and grasping as her brother, had given up her seaside boarding-house business in order to accompany Harwell in his attempts to get his hands upon the Lilliputians. But there were times when Miss Mincing wondered whether she had made the right move. She was not at all sure in her own mind that the little people really existed. She only had her brother's word for it. There were times when she wondered whether, perhaps, her brother was completely off his chump!

Harwell spun round and the smile sped from his face, glad to be gone from such alien territory. He postured in front of his sister in his oriental robes.

"I find this costume rather fetching, Sarah," he said and then added with a scowl, "but I suppose you don't approve?"

"I always knew that you were willing to go to the most extraordinary lengths, Harwell, in order to pursue your wild delusions," Sarah replied, tightlipped. "But I hardly expected to see my own brother in the Godless guise of a heathen!"

"Pah!" snarled Harwell. "There's no religious significance to the costume, Sarah, I assure you. Allow me to present myself—" He paused, drew a red silk handkerchief from a voluminous sleeve, and pulled it through his fingers where it was instantly changed into a blue one. "—Her Way Lee, oriental magician, at your service!"

"Hummmph," sniffed Sarah, unimpressed. "Harwell Mincing, charlatan and imposter more like!"

"By no means, Sarah! These clothes are genuine, as is the name—and both of them borrowed from a genuine Chinese conjuror too—a regular patron of an ale-house I frequent occasionally."

"A den of Satan. I might have guessed as much!" observed Sarah, smoothing down with her bony fingers the starched black dress she always wore.

"Hear me out, sister," Harwell said, impatiently. "I chanced to discover that the younger of the Garstanton brats is having a birthday party this afternoon. My oriental friend had been engaged to entertain at the function. So, I have conducted a small business arrangement with the gentleman, and now I shall take his place."

"You shall get your just deserts when you come finally face to face with the Devil, Harwell."

"Not so. All that are due to me are my just rewards—and I intend to collect those in this life, sister, not in the hereafter. Just as soon as I grasp those cunning little creatures in these two hands! Soon, Sarah, soon . . ."

"And how will dressing up in the outlandish garb of a heathen assist you in achieving that object?"

"It has assisted me already, Sarah, in helping me gain access to the home of the Garstanton brats."

"It won't be the first time you've crossed that particular threshold, brother," his sister pointed out, "but every time you've gone in there before, you've come out empty-handed."

Which was perfectly true. By the use of a variety of disguises, Harwell Mincing had managed to bluff his way into the Garstanton home on several previous occasions. But the little people had always seen through his ruse in time and managed to get the better of him.

"Not this time, sister," replied Harwell, and he pointed across the room at an intricately carved, red-and-gold model Chinese pagoda about forty centimetres in height, standing on a conjuror's table along with several other items of conjuring apparatus. "Not with that rather intriguing trap I've had constructed," he added.

Sarah, curious, crossed the room to examine the pagoda. "And might one enquire what it does, brother?" she asked. "Is it a simple conjuring device or—knowing you—is it something a shade more sinister?" And, as she spoke, Sarah reached out a hand towards the open arched entrance of the model temple.

"I wouldn't put my hands inside it if I were you," said Harwell. "It's hardly the place for prying fingers, believe me—there's more than one unpleasant surprise contained within those walls."

Harwell picked up a pencil from the conjuror's table, reached inside the pagoda and pressed down on the floor just inside the entrance. Immediately, a steel-barred gate shot down, snapping off the pencil's tip and sealing the pagoda's entrance.

The smile returned to Harwell's face. "There," he said, "I've had it constructed especially for the purpose of ensnaring little sly-booted creatures!"

"And just how do you propose to entice these 'little

creatures' that you talk of into your oriental prison?"

"In the same manner exactly, Sarah, that I would set out to capture any domestic rodent. I shall simply bait my trap and then allow the little creatures' natural curiosity to take its course." As he spoke, the showman lifted up the steel gate with its sharp points and re-set the hidden catch. "Oh, they'll walk into it, sister, take my word on that—as surely as flies stray on to the spider's web. And then, the moment they do . . ."

Again he pressed down, gently, just inside the pagoda entrance and, again, the steel bars shut fast and bit another two centimetres off the pencil's end.

"Hey presto!" carolled Harwell. "We shall have them!"

Sarah Mincing shuddered. "There are times, brother, when I can almost feel it in my heart to pity the poor creatures," she said, and added, "And then I find myself pitying the two of us the more."

"Pitying you and me, sister?" asked Harwell, suspiciously.

"Certainly. You for your tortured mind that first invented these little people—and me for being fool enough to listen to you in the first place."

"They exist, Sarah! Believe me, they are no figments of my imagination. And, mark my words, you'll scoff on the other side of your face before this day is through! I tell you—" But before he could tell her anything, there was a knock on the front door. "That will be the carrier I ordered, come with his cart to convey me to the party. Have him come up, Sarah, and tell him to take my conjuring apparatus down. I'll carry this for myself though." He slipped his hands underneath the pagoda, carefully. "It's far too precious to entrust to another's care."

Sarah opened the door for her brother to precede her down the stairs. Harwell Mincing set off carrying his Lilliputian trap and wearing again the self-same smile that didn't quite seem to belong on his face.

2

"Are you sure I've done it properly?" asked Philippa, looking over her shoulder in the nursery mirror at the bow she'd tied in the sash of her new party dress at the middle of her back. "Do you think I ought to try again?"

"You've tied it seven times already," said Gerald. "It's time we went downstairs, Phil—the guests will be arriving any minute."

But Philippa, not happy with her appearance, unfastened the bow and began all over again.

"I don't know why she bothers," observed Brelca grumpily, turning away from the dolls' house window through which she had been watching Philippa get ready for the party. "That dress doesn't suit her at all, you know—it would look far nicer on me."

"It wouldn't suit you either, Brelca," said Fistram, running his fingers along the painted-on keys of the dolls' house piano. "It's much too big for you."

"I'm talking about the *colour*, Fistram—not the size! *I* can get away with that shade of green—she can't."

"She's absolutely right, Fistram," observed Spelbush, staring moodily into the crinkled red crepe paper in the dolls' house fireplace which was supposed to represent a fire. "Green is a perfect match for Brelca's jealous nature."

Brelca put her tongue out at Spelbush who pretended he hadn't noticed.

But the lady Lilliputian could not be blamed if she suffered from an occasional pang of jealousy regarding clothes. Her wardrobe consisted entirely of dolls' cast-offs supplemented by one or two garments that had been run up by Philippa on her toy sewing-machine. None of them fitted. None of them were fashionable. What's more, the buttons were much too big and the stitching far too crude. None of them *looked* right.

"Clothes," sighed Brelca, half to herself, "that's what I miss the most."

"Real fires, that's what I miss," said Spelbush who, forgetting himself, had absentmindedly poked the red crepe paper with the dolls' house poker.

"Real everything," said Fistram. "A real piano with keys that play instead of just being painted on. A real front door that opens and shuts . . . instead of an entire front wall!"

His last words were addressed at the children who had just opened the front of the dolls' house and were looking down at the Lilliputians.

"I do wish people would learn some manners and have the courtesy to knock before they opened other people's homes," said Brelca with her nose in the air.

"We only wanted to tell you that it's time for us to go down to the party," said Philippa.

"We've got to be in the hall to greet the guests as they arrive," said Gerald.

"Happy birthday-party, Philippa," said Fistram.

"Have a good time," said Spelbush.

But Brelca, still cross, had turned her back towards the children.

"Don't forget the sausage-roll!" called Fistram as Gerald closed the front of the dolls' house and, just to be on the safe side, slipped home the catch.

"If that child was my daughter, I'd be *extremely* concerned," announced Brelca, huffily, as the children went out through the nursery door. "She's got no dress sense whatsoever. Did you just *see* the colour of that hair-ribbon?"

"It *is* a pity about this pretend piano," Fistram persisted. "If we had a *real* piano we could have our own party up here."

"Parties are exceedingly common, Fistram," said Brelca. "Receptions, on the other hand, are exceedingly fashionable."

"There's nothing wrong with parties, Brelca," said Fistram. "Nothing at all. We could have stood around the piano, if it worked, and sung a few songs and played a few games and eaten Madeira cake and sausage-roll . . . if we'd had any Madeira cake and sausage-roll."

"When will you learn, Fistram," snapped Brelca, "that there is nothing quite so common as sausage-rolls?"

"There's nothing common about sausage-rolls, is there, Spelbush?"

But Spelbush wasn't listening. He had slipped one end of the poker into the crack between the front of the dolls' house and the side wall. He was moving it, carefully, up and down and attempting to unhook the catch that held the dolls' house shut fast. It was a trick that he had learned some months before and one of which the children were not aware.

"Where are you going, Spelbush?" asked Brelca as she heard the click of the catch which signified that Spelbush had been successful.

17

"Downstairs, of course. To the party."

"I thought we agreed with the children that we'd keep out of trouble and stay up here?" said Fistram, anxiously, believing that any breach of the rules might put an end to the possibility of Madeira cake or pink blancmange arriving from the birthday feast.

"No. *You* agreed to stay up here, Fistram," Spelbush reminded his companion. "*I* said I wanted to see the Chinese conjuror—all you were interested in, as usual, was your stomach." With which, he put all his weight against the inside of the front wall of the dolls' house and pushed, hard. "Coming, Brelca?" he asked, as the wall began to move.

Brelca nodded, happily. The two of them walked out of the dolls' house on to the nursery floor.

"You said you wouldn't be caught dead at a children's party!" Fistram shouted after Brelca.

"I don't intend to be caught at all!" she called back over her shoulder. "I shall keep very much out of sight!"

"*And* you said that parties were common!"

"They *are* common. But the very fact that I shall be attending it, Fistram," replied Brelca, "will give it just that little touch of class."

"Wait for me!" called Fistram, who had no wish to be left out of things. "I'm coming too!"

And he set off, at a run, to join the other two who were already on their way through the half-open nursery door.

The Lilliputians negotiated the bedroom stairs in their usual manner—easily and swiftly, using each others' backs as stepping-stones. They paused on the first-floor landing and peered down through the banister rails into the hall where the young guests were beginning to arrive.

Millie relieved a couple of newly arrived children of their hats and coats and then turned to where Gerald and Philippa were standing. "Look sharp, you two!" she said. "H'escort Miss h'Emma and Master h'Alexander up to the parlour then!"

As the four children moved off up the stairs, the housemaid who had brought the two new guests turned to Millie.

"What time am I supposed to collect 'em, Mill?" she asked.

"Carriages h'is requested for a quarter to seven sharp, h'Agnes," said Millie, primly. Then, lowering her voice, she added, "But if you gets 'ere a bit before'and, gel, you'll drop in lucky for some left-overs. There en'arf been a spread laid on!"

The three Lilliputians had had the good sense to make themselves scarce long before the children arrived on the landing. Gerald and Philippa and the two guests paused to tiptoe into the dining room and admire the food on the table.

"We're not supposed to come in here yet," said Philippa, hungrily.

"It's games first," explained Gerald, "in the parlour."

"Will there be Pass-the-Parcel?" asked Emma.

"And Spin-the-Bottle?" asked Alexander.

Philippa nodded vigorously. "And Pin-the-Tail-on-the-Donkey and Hunt-the-Thimble," she said.

"And then it's in here for tea," said Gerald.

"And after tea it's the Chinese conjuror," said Philippa.

Gerald glanced anxiously towards the landing at the sound of more knocking at the front door. "That's someone else arriving," she said. "We'd better get out of here before Grandfather comes in."

Brelca and Spelbush waited until the children had gone before walking out from behind the big bowl of trifle where they had been hiding.

"Where's Fistram?" said Spelbush.

Brelca glanced around in surprise. "I thought he was with us," she said.

Spelbush let out a little sigh and shook his head in mild exasperation. "Look!" he said, pointing across at a huge pink blancmange that was trembling visibly.

"We might have guessed as much!" said Brelca.

They tiptoed across the snow-white tablecloth and peered round the blancmange. Fistram was perched on the edge of the plate, nibbling contentedly at a handful of the decorative piped white-cream edging which he had pulled off. Brelca and Spelbush shook their heads at Fistram in disgust.

"Have some," he said. "it's very good."

Outside in the street, a horse-drawn hansom cab had pulled up and more guests were getting down.

A couple of street urchins were standing on the pavement enjoying the excitement of watching the comings and goings outside the Garstanton home.

" 'Ave you ever been to a party, 'orace?" asked the larger boy.

The smaller, Horace, who was holding an empty jug, shook his head. "No," he replied. "But I went on a Sunday School outing once—on a n'orse'n cart."

"You never?" said the first urchin in some surprise. "I didn't know you'd been to Sunday School?"

"I 'aven't," said the smaller of the two. "I climbed up on the cart when nobody was looking."

"Listen!" said the first urchin, glancing up at the first-floor window.

Grandfather Garstanton had struck up a thumping tune on the piano in the parlour where several children were now assembled. The party was getting under way.

"Crikey Moses!" exclaimed the smaller street urchin. "Look at that!"

The larger boy followed his companion's glance. As the hansom cab moved off along the street, a horse-drawn van pulled up outside the Garstanton house. Sitting up on the driving-seat, next to the van-driver, was a man in Chinese robes wearing a long drooping moustache.

"What abaht 'im then!" breathed the smaller urchin, blinking in wide-eyed wonder at this latest arrival. But the boy was not to be allowed to enjoy the treat of admiring the spectacle for long. "Ooh-er!" he cried as a hand took hold of his left ear and squeezed, hard.

"Where's my ale?" growled an angry voice he recognized all too well.

"Ow! *Don't!*" moaned the lad as the hand squeezed harder still and his head was twisted round until his eyes were staring up into the face of the man who held him fast. "I was just going for your beer, Dad—'onest I was!"

"Just going? Are you telling me, your father, that you 'aven't even fetched it yet, you good-for-nothing tyke!" As he spoke, the man snatched the empty jug from the boy's hand and raised it, threateningly. "I've a good mind to—"

"I only stopped for a minute, Dad," wailed the urchin,

twisting and turning helplessly in his father's unrelenting grip. "Just outside this 'ouse to watch the toffs turn up—"

"It's true what your 'orace says, Mister Dobson," put in the taller urchin. "We was just off to fetch your beer, 'onest to God—"

"Only there's this Chinaman—look—" added the smaller of the two.

"I'll give you toffs and Chinamen, my lad!" snarled his father. "Get off 'ome—I'll fetch my own beer. Go on, scarper—before I . . ."

The two boys took to their heels and fled along the street.

While all this was going on, Harwell and the van-driver had got down and were unloading the magical apparatus on to the pavement.

"Give you a 'and to carry your goods, sir?" said the man called Dobson, putting on an oily, cringing expression as he approached Harwell. "I'll 'old your 'orse for you for sixpence."

"Be off with you, scoundrel," growled Harwell. "Before I summon a constable and have you taken in charge!"

Dobson paused only long enough to glance greedily at the red-and-gold pagoda which Harwell was lifting out of the back of the van. "I'll bet that's worth a shilling or two," he mumbled to himself as he slunk off along the street in the direction of the ale-house.

Harwell turned to the van-driver. "Take all these things inside the house," he said, curtly. "And then you can go—but see that you're back here to collect me on the stroke of seven."

"Right you are, guv'nor," said the van-driver.

Harwell knocked on the front door of the Garstanton house. He smoothed his oriental robes with his hands and

adopted what he imagined to be a suitably oriental expression. The door opened and Millie peered out. She blinked
and gulped at the sight of the tall Chinaman on her
doorstep.

"Gleetings, honolable missie!" warbled Harwell in what
he considered to be an oriental accent.

" 'Ow d'yer do, y'r 'ighness!" stuttered Millie, who had
been seized by a sudden attack of the goose-bumps at the
encounter. And then, collecting herself, she flung the front
door wide open, curtsied, and continued in her best
housemaid's manner, "Do come in—you h'are
h'expected—an' there's a cold rice-pudden in the larder!"

"Lawks-a-mercy!" exclaimed Millie as she surveyed the
dining table. "They ain't left much in the way of left-overs!
You'd think 'arf of Kitchener's army 'ad been in 'ere for a
tuck-in—not just a gang of kids!"

Which was no great exaggeration. The party guests had
sat down and set to and put away Cook's spread with gusto.
You would have thought that not one of them had been fed
for a fortnight. Every last jam tart was gone. Every single
maid-of-honour had been hungrily consumed. Every single
slice of cake had slipped down somebody's throat. Every
butterfly bun had flown. There was nothing left but
crumbs—and not too many of them!

Millie shook her head in disbelief. "I'll come in and clear
up later," she murmured to herself as she bustled from the
dining room.

As soon as the maid was gone, the three Lilliputians
moved out from their hiding-place behind the sideboard.
They too surveyed the empty table.

"So much for pink blancmange," sighed Fistram, ruefully. "I *knew* those children wouldn't leave us anything! Did you ever *see* anyone eat so fast?"

"Yes," said Brelca. "You—given half a chance."

"Can't you forget your stomach just this once, Fistram?" said Spelbush. "You eat three good meals every day—"

"He eats *all* day every day," put in Brelca.

Spelbush frowned at Brelca at this interruption and then continued to Fistram, "—how often do you get the chance to watch a real live Chinese conjuror?"

"I bet he can't make things vanish as quickly as those sausage-rolls disappeared," muttered Fistram.

"Shut up!" said Spelbush. "And come along!" With which, he set off across the dining-room carpet towards the door which had been left ajar by Millie.

But as the Lilliputians came out on to the first-floor landing they were shocked to discover that the parlour door was shut tight.

"What do we do now?" asked Brelca.

"A fine party this is turning out to be for us!" snapped Fistram. "First no food and now no conjuror either!" And he sat down sulkily at the top of the stairs and sank his chin on his fists.

"Get up!" hissed Spelbush. "Somebody's coming!"

Fistram scrambled to his feet hastily, and joined his companions as they scuttled across the landing and took refuge underneath a cupboard.

"Do 'urry, Cook!" said Millie, scampering up from downstairs. "We'll miss the magic!"

"What's going to happen to all that washing-up in the kitchen, that's what *I'd* like to know!" said Cook. "There's no magician going to wave a magic wand and get that done."

"Oh—bother the washing-up!" said Millie. "There's a party going on—we've been h'officially h'invited!" She knocked on the parlour door, gently, then opened it and peered inside.

The heavy velvet window curtains had been drawn, shutting out the late afternoon light. A number of oil-lamps had been arranged at one end of the room where two screens were set up to represent a little stage. There were two black conjuror's tables in front of these screens. On one of the tables were a number of mysterious boxes and other items appertaining to the art of magic. On the second table stood the red-and-gold Chinese pagoda. The party guests were sitting on the rows of chairs patiently waiting for the entertainment to begin. But there was no sign, as yet, of the Chinese conjuror.

"Come in, Millie! Come in, Cook!" called Mr Garstanton who was standing at the back of the room with his camera and flash equipment at the ready. "You're just in time to be amazed!" he added.

Millie held the door open wide for Cook to enter.

At the same moment, taking advantage of the opportunity, the three little people darted out from underneath the cupboard, ran across the landing and into the parlour before Millie had time to close the door. Unnoticed, they slipped beneath the nearest chair. Then, in the half-darkness, they crept forward through the forest of children's legs until they were in the very front row.

"The best seats in the house!" whispered Brelca, squatting on the parlour floor.

"I wonder what that does?" queried Fistram, pointing up at the red-and-gold pagoda.

"It probably vanishes things," said Brelca.

25

"Sssshhhh!" Spelbush cautioned them, putting a finger to his lips. "If anyone finds us here, we're done for!"

But there was no need for the warning. Brelca and Fistram lapsed into total silence as the Chinese conjuror appeared from behind one of the screens. His face glowed eerily in the soft light from the oil-lamps. His long thin shiny black moustache hung down inscrutably on either side of his mouth. His dark eyes peered sinisterly all around the room.

"Do you know something," said Brelca, in puzzled tones. "I think I've seen him somewhere before?"

"Oh, *do* be quiet!" hissed Spelbush.

The Chinese conjuror's hands fluttered mysteriously as he reached up and plucked a colourful silk scarf out of thin air.

A chorus of "Ooohs!" rose from the audience.

The Chinese conjuror's long fingers performed more mystical passes and this time he produced a large oriental fan from out of nowhere.

The audience once more let out a chorus of "Aaahs!"

Harwell Mincing, it should be explained, had spent some time studying magic with the real Chinese conjuror and he had learned his lessons well.

His fingers danced and weaved over the top of the red-and-gold pagoda. There came, it seemed, the tinkling sound of oriental bells from inside the Chinese temple. The conjuror pulled from the gilded roof a giant bouquet of flowers fashioned out of feathers, then more silk squares and, finally, a real goldfish bowl with a real, live goldfish swimming inside it.

The audience clapped its hands and uttered more delighted "Ooohs!" and "Aaahs!"

Fistram, however, was not impressed. "It's all done with mirrors, you know," he announced.

"Ssshhhh!" whispered Spelbush and Brelca in unison.

Harwell Mincing, having finished his magic with the red-and-gold pagoda, lifted the model off the table and set it down in the shadows on the floor. Nobody heard the tiny "Click!" as he pressed the switch that set the trap inside the entrance to the pagoda.

Moving back into the light from the oil-lamps, the Chinese conjuror picked up a large black box from the other table.

He lifted off the lid and showed the inside of the box to the audience to prove that it was empty. He put the lid back on the box. He tapped the lid with his magic wand. He lifted off the lid again.

Hey presto!

Suddenly, the box was full!

Flags-of-all-nations; a string of fake sausages; still *more* silk handkerchiefs; vast showers of playing-cards—there was no end, it seemed, to what the box could hold. And, finally, when every single member of the audience was sure at last that the conjuror had exhausted the box's secret contents, he plunged his hand in for a final time and pulled out a kicking, twitching, snow-white rabbit.

There were more "Oooohs!" and "Aaaahs!" and still more applause.

Everyone was entranced by the conjuror's show. Everyone, that is, except for one of the Lilliputians hidden beneath the front row of chairs.

Fistram, who was always quickly bored by any form of entertainment that had nothing to do with food, was sitting twiddling his thumbs and clicking his tongue, loudly, against the roof of his mouth in order to make his feelings known.

"Be quiet, Fistram!" snapped Brelca.

"It's done with mirrors, I tell you," replied Fistram, pointing towards the conjuror.

"Hush!" said Spelbush.

"It's either done with mirrors," said Fistram, airily, "or he's got things hidden up his sleeve—that's why Chinese conjurors have such wide sleeves, you know—so they can hide things up them."

"SSSHHHH!" hissed Spelbush and Brelca in unison.

They turned their attention back to the conjuror who was now magicking a fluttering grey dove out of a shining omelette-pan which, they could have sworn, had been quite empty only an instant before.

"Where's Fistram?" asked Spelbush with a frown, glancing around as soon as the trick was over and spotting the empty place beside him.

Fistram, it seemed, had done a vanishing trick of his own!

"Over there!" gasped Brelca.

Their companion was ambling unconcernedly across the parlour carpet in the direction of the red-and-gold pagoda which the conjuror had placed on the floor. Luckily, the carpet was in shadow and not one of the party guests had spotted the little man strolling across the floor.

"What's he up to now?" muttered Spelbush, getting to his feet. "Come on! We'd better fetch him back before he gets into *more* trouble."

Fistram had stopped and was staring hard at the dark, arched entrance of the pagoda. The gentle sound of temple bells was still tinkling mysteriously from somewhere deep inside.

Now this *was* interesting, he thought. Much better than the conjuror. And who could say what good things might be contained within the pagoda's walls? Sweets, perhaps? Hidden away for the conjuror to produce later in the show and hand out as treats to the party guests? It was not impossible. It was certainly worth investigating.

Fistram took a step nearer the dark archway.

"Fistram!" snapped Spelbush, at his elbow. "What do you think you're up to?"

"I'm going to have a look inside."

"What for?" demanded Brelca, who had also caught up with Fistram.

"Er . . . I'm going to prove to you that it's all done with mirrors," replied Fistram, cagily. He had decided not to tell his friends that he was really looking for something to eat. "Are you coming with me or staying here?"

Brelca and Spelbush exchanged a doubtful look, but decided to go with him all the same. There *was*, they were forced to admit, something rather intriguing about the pagoda.

But there was something suspicious about it too, Spelbush decided as soon as he stepped through the archway. "Let's get out of here," he said with a shiver.

In front of them was a dark corridor around the end of which was an eerie red and orange glow.

"Go back? What on earth *for*?" demanded Fistram, who was already several paces ahead of his companions.

"Spelbush is right," said Brelca, who was standing behind Spelbush and peering over his shoulder. "I don't

29

think we should go any further either—I don't think it's safe."

They could hear the temple bells much clearer now. But what had sounded like a welcoming tinkle outside, now seemed more like the clanging toll of a warning bell.

"What are you both afraid of?" scoffed Fistram. "It's only a conjuror's box after all—a thing of paint and wood. We might find something good to eat around the corner—" In his excitement, Fistram had given away the reason why he had decided to investigate the inside of the pagoda.

"So *that's* what it is!" grumbled Spelbush.

"We might have guessed it!" added Brelca.

"Your greed, Fistram," went on Spelbush, sternly, "will land us in *real* trouble one of these fine days—"

Spelbush's warning came true before he even had time to finish the sentence. To their dismay, they heard the steel-barred gate slam shut behind them. Fistram, taking one step too many, had stepped on the hidden switch that controlled the mechanism over the entrance.

The three Lilliputians spun round at the sound and stared at the steel bars, horror-struck. They ran back along the corridor, took hold of the bars and shook them, fiercely. But it was no use. They realized at once that they were trapped.

"We're doomed," said Fistram, in a small sad voice, knowing that, in part at least, he was to blame for their predicament.

"Look!" said Spelbush, pointing through the bars.

The other two followed his gaze.

A familiar shoe was peeping out from beneath the Chinese conjuror's long robe.

"Where have you seen *that* foot before?" said Spelbush.

"Harwell Mincing!" gasped Brelca. "We might have guessed!"

The little people had had several brushes with the cunning showman. It was not the first time that he had resorted to disguise in his attempts to trap them. But on every previous occasion, despite their size, the Lilliputians had managed to get the better of their enemy. This time, alas, it looked as if Harwell Mincing had won at last.

"Now what?" said Brelca, looking to Spelbush for advice.

"That's easy!" It was Fistram who replied. "We shout for help."

With which, he opened his mouth wide but Spelbush clapped a hand across his face before he could utter a sound.

"We can't do that," he said, nodding across at the rows of seated party guests. All this time, of course, the children had been watching the conjuror's magic, with no inkling of the drama that was taking place on the parlour floor. "If we call out now," continued Spelbush, "we will give our secret away for ever."

"It's either that or leave ourselves in that rascal's hands," said Fistram.

Brelca shook her head. "Spelbush is right," she said. "We're not beaten yet . . ." She paused to peer back along the dark and gloomy corridor which led into the pagoda, ". . . at least, not quite . . ." she added in a tiny voice.

"It's time for us to do some investigating," said Spelbush, briskly, in an attempt to bolster his companions' spirits—although, truth to tell, he would have liked someone to have bolstered his own! "Follow me," he said.

Then, trying to hide his own doubts and sinking feelings,

Spelbush led Fistram and Brelca along the corridor towards the orange glow.

3

*"Welcome little ones! Try not to be
impatient—it will not be long now
before we meet each other face to face."*

The words were painted in a kind of oriental lettering on
the red-and-gold wall of the main room of the pagoda.
From either side of this painted message, the frightening
painted face of an oriental god frowned down on the three
Lilliputians. These two glowering faces seemed almost to
come alive in the flickering orange light that came from the
smouldering incense sticks burning on a small carved altar
in the centre of the room.

There was no sound now inside the Chinese pagoda. The
temple bells had stopped their ringing at the very moment
the steel gate slammed shut.

One thing, at least, was obvious to the Lilliputians as
they gazed around the room—there was only one way out
of the pagoda and that was through the archway which was
now barred to them. The carpenter who had constructed
the oriental trap for Harwell Mincing had performed his
task well.

"*Now* what do you propose we do?" said Fistram, looking
at Spelbush.

Spelbush shrugged. He tried to look unconcerned and as

if he had things well in control. "Get some rest," he said, lowering himself on to the pagoda floor. "The next move now is up to Harwell Mincing."

At that moment, there came a burst of applause from the parlour.

Harwell Mincing, keeping one eye on the pagoda, had heard and seen the tiny metal-barred gate slam. He knew that the Lilliputians were now his prisoners. He was bringing his magic show to an end.

The children clapped and clapped as he performed his final trick involving a large wooden dice which kept mysteriously vanishing and reappearing inside a gaily painted wooden box.

Then, as the Chinese conjuror took his bow, Philippa and Gerald cheered as loudly as any of their guests.

"This is the best birthday party I've ever had," whispered Philippa, turning to her brother.

Gerald nodded. "I wish *they* could have come down and watched it though," he said, meaningfully, nodding up at the nursery which was above their heads. "They would have enjoyed themselves."

Outside the front door of the Garstanton house, the van-man was lounging against the shafts of his cart with a yellow-stained clay pipe clamped between his teeth.

"Move yourself, fellow!" snarled Harwell as he bustled out into the street, hugging the Chinese pagoda to his chest. "The rest of my things are in the hall."

The van-driver stuck his pipe into his waistcoat pocket, tipped his cap at Harwell and moved to obey.

"At last, my little wanderers!" crooned Harwell, softly, through the barred entrance of the pagoda. "After all these long months of waiting, I hold you in these hands!" With which, and loath to put his prized possession down, he clambered up on to the seat, still clutching it tight.

Inside the hall, as the party guests put on hats and boots and coats, and the van-man bustled to and fro with the conjuring equipment, Millie turned to greet Agnes, her fellow housemaid, who had arrived to collect her two young charges.

"What a pity you couldn't 'ave come 'ere sooner, Aggie," said Millie. "That there Chinese conjuror was a real right proper treat an' no mistake!" Then she paused and frowned as she remembered something. " 'E's gorn off without eating 'is rice-pudden though, what Cook put out for 'im. 'E's in a bit of a 'urry, it seems. Shame, innit?"

And Agnes nodded in agreement as she helped Emma and Alexander into their things.

"Quick as you can, fellow," snapped Harwell.

The van-driver loaded the last of the conjuring tricks into the back of his van, clambered up beside Harwell and cracked his whip.

The horse tugged between the shafts and the van rattled off along the cobbled street.

The journey did not take long. Minutes later, the van pulled up outside the dingy entrance to Harwell's favourite ale-house.

"I shall be two minutes at the very most," he growled at the van-man as he lowered himself to the ground. "Do not allow your eyes to stray from that for so much as a second," he added, nodding at the pagoda which he had placed on the seat.

"Trust me, guv!" said the van-man, reaching into his waistcoat pocket for his stub of a pipe.

35

Once inside the ale-house, Harwell Mincing blinked his eyes in order to accustom them to the smoke-filled gloom. The ale-house was a well-known meeting-place for thieves and ne'er-do-wells and rogues where strange disguises were commonplace. Harwell's Chinese costume caused little interest among the regular customers.

Spotting who he was looking for, Harwell crossed to a quiet corner table where a *real* Chinaman was drinking alone.

Harwell sat down beside him. "Congratulations, Way Lee," he said. "You are an excellent tutor—the entertainment was an unqualified success."

The Chinaman who was, of course, a true conjuror and the owner of the magic tricks and oriental costume, said nothing. He nodded, gravely, sipped at his drink and examined his long thin fingers one by one.

"I believe that half a sovereign was the price we agreed," continued Harwell, reaching into his robes and taking out his purse.

Before opening it though, he glanced around the ale-house to make sure that his business was being conducted unobserved. There was no cause for alarm. The regular patrons were all far too busy plotting their own misdeeds to pay any attention to the two men at the corner table.

At the bar, the landlord wiped his hands on his grubby apron and shook his bald head. "Sorry, Silas," he said. "You know my rules—no money, no ale. In any event, you've had more than enough for one evening."

The man snarled an oath and staggered from the bar, taking with him an empty jug. He peered across at Harwell as he blundered towards the door.

The man tried to pull his muddled thoughts together. He

was sure he'd seen the man in Chinese robes before. Had he not had quite so much to drink he would have remembered where. They had crossed each other's paths earlier that self-same evening—in Victoria Street outside the old photographer's house.

The drunken man was Silas Dobson, the father of Horace Dobson, the street urchin who had stopped with his companion to watch the arrival of the party guests and the unloading of the horse-drawn van.

But Dobson's mind was too befuddled now to recall events of several hours before. He shook his head, giving up the attempt, and continued his unsteady progress towards the door, cursing under his breath again as he stumbled against a wooden stool which he then kicked out of his way.

Once outside, the cool air cleared his head a little. He blinked and frowned as he saw, first, the horse-van parked outside in the street and, next, the red-and-gold pagoda standing unattended on the driving-seat.

The van-driver, disregarding Harwell's orders to keep his eyes on the pagoda, had got down on to the pavement and was leaning against the side of his van, enjoying a quiet smoke.

Silas Dobson sobered all the more as he stared, enviously, at the red-and-gold pagoda. He had wanted it when he first spied it being carried into the Garstanton home—now as it stood there for the taking, he desired it all the more.

The van-man, fussing with his pipe, had not seen Dobson stagger out of the ale-house. He did not see him now as he crept, still a shade unsteadily, around and behind the back of the van. Once there, Silas Dobson drew back his arm and flung the jug along the empty street as far as he was able. It crashed on the cobbles, shattering noisily into a thousand pieces.

The van-driver, puzzled at the sound, set off along the street to investigate the cause. Dobson, seizing his chance, snatched up the red-and-gold pagoda and, staggering under its weight, set off in the opposite direction where he was quickly swallowed up by the darkness.

"It was the nicest—the *best*—the *very* best birthday party that there ever was, Grandfather," said Philippa, contentedly.

"I'm pleased that you enjoyed it, child," said Mr Garstanton, standing at the door of the nursery. "Let's hope that next year your mama and papa are here to share it with you. I'll be up again later to bid you both goodnight."

As soon as their grandfather had gone, closing the nursery door behind him, the children revealed to each other the things they had had hidden behind their backs.

"A whole custard tart and half a sausage-roll," said Gerald, holding them up for his sister's approval. "What did you manage?"

"A slice of Madeira cake and a piece of apple-pie," replied Philippa, carefully unwrapping the handkerchief in which they were contained.

The children smiled at each other, satisfied with their haul, then turned towards the dolls' house where, they imagined, their little guests would be waiting to enjoy the feast.

The smile faded fast from both their faces. The front of the dolls' house stood open wide.

The Lilliputians weren't inside.

"Fistram? Spelbush!" cried Gerald, peering around the nursery floor.

"Brelca?" called Philippa, dropping to her knees and searching behind the coal scuttle. But it was all too quickly obvious that the little people were nowhere in the nursery. "They've gone, Gerald!" she wailed.

"They *can't* have gone," replied her brother, puzzled. "They must be *somewhere*."

"They've gone," said Philippa again, this time in a hollow, hopeless voice. She tried hard to blink back the tear that was creeping out of the corner of one eye. "I *know* they've gone. I just *know* it, Gerald."

The three Lilliputians clung grimly to whatever hand-holds they could find as the pagoda lurched violently up and down. Hot ashes spilled from the altar fire and tumbled dangerously around their feet. They could hear, from outside, the laboured panting of Silas Dobson and the clatter of his boots along the cobbles as he stumbled through the empty streets.

"Hold on, Brelca!" called Spelbush, as yet another shower of sparks and glowing ashes shot across the floor.

"Yes, Brelca—hold on tight!" cried Fistram.

Brelca nodded, dumbly, and held on as tight as she was able.

Then, all at once, the movement stopped.

Silas Dobson, completely exhausted, was standing in the centre of the street and gulping in great mouthfuls of air. Directly in front of him there stood open the ornate, cast-iron gates of a public park. Carrying the pagoda with some care, Dobson set off into the park.

Several streets away, outside the ale-house, Harwell

39

Mincing peered into the darkness and turned, angrily, to the van-man. "You oaf!" he roared. "You clumsy incompetent oaf! I told you not to take your eyes from it!"

" 'Tworn't my fault," grumbled the van-driver, climbing up into his driving-seat. "What was it anyway? 'Tworn't worth nothing—'tworn't no more'n a bit of a painted wooden box."

"The contents of that painted wooden box, man, were more valuable than precious stones! Would that I had a wooden box now that was large enough to contain thy useless carcass!" stormed Harwell, as he clambered up beside the van-man. "Drive on then, fool," he muttered. "Drive on—we'll find the thief if it means we have to search the streets all night!"

The van-man flicked his whip and the horse and van and occupants clattered off again into the night.

In the very centre of Holdsworth Park stood an imposing statue of the portly, bewhiskered Josiah Holdsworth, factory owner and civic benefactor, in whose honour the park had been named.

It was at the foot of this statue that Silas Dobson chose to sit in the moonlight and examine his prize. He lifted the pagoda up to his face and, in an attempt to guess at what it might contain, shook the wooden model hard.

Inside the pagoda, the sudden movement caused all three of the Lilliputians to lose their grip and roll around the floor.

"There's summat inside there for sure!" Dobson muttered to himself. He set the pagoda down on the stone step that ran round the base of the statue. He tugged and pulled at the wooden roof with both his hands. But to no avail.

40

"An' whatever it is that's in there must be worth a sovereign or two," he reasoned to himself, "or why else would they keep the accursed thing locked tight?"

Then, giving up his attempt to tear open the roof, he switched his attention to the archway entrance. Dobson slipped his forefinger through the steel bars. Unwittingly, he touched the secret catch on the pagoda floor.

The steel-barred gate shot open.

"Ah—now for it!" he chuckled, rolling up his sleeve before thrusting his hand and wrist along the corridor.

Inside, the three Lilliputians shrank back as Dobson's hand appeared and moved around, feeling the walls and floor. Spelbush and Fistram, hugging the rear wall, managed to keep out of reach of the groping hand. But Brelca, alas, had chosen to flee in the wrong direction and found herself held fast between a giant thumb and forefinger.

"What's this then?" they heard Dobson mumble to himself. "Almost feels as if it was alive!"

Brelca pushed and wriggled and squirmed in her efforts to free herself from the tight grip that was tugging her nearer and nearer towards the pagoda's entrance.

"Hold fast, Brelca!" cried Spelbush and, dashing forward, he snatched up a burning incense stick out of the altar fire and plunged the glowing end into the ball of Dobson's thumb. Fistram, taking his cue from Spelbush, also grabbed at a burning brand and jabbed it, hard, at the top knuckle of Dobson's forefinger.

"Oooooh!" yelled Silas Dobson, and, "Aaaaah!" he went, as the glowing sticks stabbed into his flesh. He loosed his hold on Brelca at once and snatched his hand out of the pagoda. "It *is* alive!" he cried. "It bit me! The damned thing bit me!"

41

Then, gazing down at the pagoda, fearful at what strange and dangerous animal might be contained within its walls, he backed slowly away across the park. Only when he considered that he had put a sufficiently safe distance between himself and it, did he dare to turn his back on the pagoda and flee from the scene as fast as he was able.

Hearing his footsteps fading in the distance, the three little people waited several minutes more, just to make sure that all was safe, and then they walked out along the corridor, through the pagoda's archway, into the moonlit night.

The dark grey statue of Josiah Holdsworth loomed up, as far as Lilliputian eye could see, above their heads.

Far away, beyond the impenetrable jungle of towering stalks in a nearby flowerbed, they could see a black mass of trees that seemed to stretch away for ever.

"Wooo-Hooooo!" hooted an owl in one of those far-off trees.

Brelca, Fistram and Spelbush, lost and unprotected in the giants' world of Holdsworth Park, shivered as they held their breaths and edged a little closer together.

4

"I, Spelbush Frelock, master navigator and sole surviving officer of the *Antelope* expedition," quavered Spelbush, taking a nervous step forward and raising a shaking right hand, "do hereby name these situate territories Quinbus Interior, in the name of his most mighty majesty, Emperor Golbasto Momaren—" Spelbush broke off to glance round at his two companions who were standing just behind him and eyeing him curiously. "You two as well—raise your elbows," he said.

Brelca and Fistram exchanged a doubtful glance but did as Spelbush had ordered, saluting in Lilliputian fashion.

". . . do hereby name these situate territories Quinbus Interior," Spelbush began again, "in the name of his most mighty majesty, Emperor Golbasto Momaren Evlame Gurdilo *etcetera etcetera*—"

"Spelbush!" snapped Brelca, deciding that enough was enough and lowering her hand. "This is hardly the time for any of your *etcera etcetering*!"

"Don't interrupt me now, Brelca," replied Spelbush, fussily. "Not when I'm declaring sovereignty—it's an extremely important ceremony."

"But is it absolutely necessary to do it *now*, Spelbush?" said Fistram, taking Brelca's side in the argument.

Spelbush let out a long-suffering sigh and lowered his

right hand. "Have either of you two got the faintest idea where we are?" he asked.

Fistram and Brelca gazed around the moonlit vast expanse that was Holdsworth Park and shook their heads.

"There you are then!" exclaimed Spelbush, triumphantly.

"*Where?*" demanded Fistram and Brelca in unison.

"If I name these situate territories Quinbus Interior," Spelbush patiently explained, "we'll know *exactly* where we are—we'll be in Quinbus Interior—not only that, instead of being in an alien terrain, we'll be standing on our own native territory—"

"Wooo-HoooOOO!"

Spelbush broke off his curious train of thought as the owl, which had hooted some minutes before, hooted again.

"If you're our leader—lead us!" said Brelca, turning to Spelbush who had almost jumped out of his skin at the sound of the owl-hoot and was now shivering behind her back. "Get us out of here," she added.

Fistram, who was still carrying his incense-stick sword, placed the weapon in Spelbush's hand and then patted the hand, encouragingly. "Go on, Spelbush," he said, echoing Brelca's words. "Lead us!"

Spelbush glanced hesitantly around the moonlit park. "Which way?" he asked.

"You're supposed to be the master navigator, you tell us!" said Brelca, sharply.

"I can't navigate without my charts and instruments," argued Spelbush. "Where are we heading for, anyway?"

"If you don't know how to get us there, Spelbush," began Brelca, heatedly, "where we're heading for is of small importance!"

"Oh, do stop *arguing*, you two!" pleaded Fistram. "It doesn't matter *where* we go—or which direction we take to get there—" he paused and glanced back over his shoulder at the red-and-gold pagoda which had recently been their prison, "—just so long as we get away from *here*!"

"On the other hand, if we stay put," Spelbush pointed out, "the children might come and find us."

"They *might*—provided Harwell Mincing doesn't get here first," said Brelca.

Spelbush took the point. "This way!" he announced, holding his incense-stick sword aloft. He strode out towards the flowerbed jungle.

Brelca and Fistram fell into step behind him.

They travelled in single file, marching first across a plain of well-trimmed lawn. Spelbush paused once only in the trek across the smooth green surface and that was in order to look up at a huge sign which towered over their heads.

"What does it say?" asked Fistram.

Spelbush waited for the moon to come out from behind a cloud before he studied the words printed on the metal hoarding. "It says *Keep off the Grass*," he told them, softly, adding, "But I don't think that we need worry about it."

Not long after this brief stop, the three little people arrived at the first fringe of stalks which marked the entrance to the flowerbed. They were pleased to discover that the bulbs had not been planted as closely together as appeared from a distance. And, although it was quite dark inside the jungle—for the moon could not penetrate the thick curtain of blooms above the travellers' heads—it was not too difficult to force a path through the stalks, brushing back a stray leaf or pushing aside a weed that blocked their way.

45

The Lilliputians, travelling in silence, made good progress and it was not too long before they caught a glimpse of moonlight through the stalks ahead.

Minutes later, they stepped out into open country again.

Spelbush held up a hand and came to a sudden halt. He stopped *so* suddenly, in fact, that Brelca bumped into him from behind, causing Fistram to bump into her.

"Now what?" asked Brelca, crossly, having received two bumps to her companions' one apiece. "What have we stopped for *this* time?"

"Look there!" said Spelbush, pointing to a huge dark shape in front of them. "There's a hill ahead—do we climb over or walk around it?"

"Around it would be easier," said Fistram.

"Over it would be quicker though," said Brelca. "And once we're on the top we'll be able to spy out what lies ahead. It isn't very steep, Spelbush—lead on."

And they set off again, Spelbush striking ahead, scrambling and scrabbling their way up the foothills towards the summit.

"Hold on!" called Spelbush, coming to a halt for a third time—but, having learned his lesson, he did not pull up quite so sharply as before.

"What is it now?" asked Brelca.

Spelbush glanced back at his companions nervously. "Didn't you feel anything?" he said.

"Feel what?"

"The earth—it moved beneath my feet."

"Nonsense!" snapped Brelca. "I didn't feel anything."

Fistram twitched. "I did!" he said. "It happened again—just then. It was an earth-tremor."

Then, all at once, there could be no doubt of it—the

ground beneath their feet began to rise up sharply.

"It's more than a tremor!" cried Spelbush, horrified. "It's an entire earthquake!"

"*Help!*" cried Fistram, in fear and trembling.

His panic was justified. The entire land mass beneath them shifted, rising up and throwing the little people, all three, off their balance, sending them tumbling down the hill to end up sprawling on the grass.

Then, to their horror, as they got to their feet, they saw a huge unshaven dirty face staring down at them.

What they had taken to be a hill was no such thing. The great dark mass had proved to be a tramp who, having had too much to drink, had stretched himself out in the grass to sleep himself sober. Having been disturbed by the tickle of Lilliputian feet across his stomach, he had pulled himself up on to one ragged elbow and was now blinking down, bleary-eyed, at the little people, unable to believe what he saw.

In their turn, Spelbush, Fistram and Brelca stood frozen to the spot with fear.

Still half-drunk, and still half-asleep, the tramp poked an unsteady forefinger at the little people. If he could touch them, he told himself, then they must be real. If he could not touch them, of course, it would mean that there was nothing there and he was seeing things. The forefinger hovered in the air as the tramp hesitated before making the final prod that might prove he was going mad.

The trembling finger hanging close to his face galvanized Spelbush into action. "Run!" he cried. "Run, Brelca! Run, Fistram!"

What the hovering finger had done for Spelbush, Spelbush's voice did for his two companions. No longer were they rooted to the spot. The three Lilliputians turned tail and fled into the darkness, running back the way they had come.

The tramp blinked his eyes and shook his head in an attempt to clear his mind. He stared hard at the spot where the three little folk had stood. But now there was nothing at all. He picked up from the grass the bottle which he had emptied only a few short hours before. Alcohol, he told himself, did peculiar things to people.

Scrambling to his feet, the tramp tossed the empty bottle into some nearby bushes. As he staggered off across the park, he promised himself that it would be many a long day before he touched strong drink again.

The sun had edged up over the roof-tops and was peering through the lace curtains into the parlour of the Garstanton home. Millie was clearing out the previous night's ashes from the grate.

Millie Lottersby was an early riser. "Lose an hour in the morning, Millie gel," she often told herself, "an' you'll spend all day looking for it." Millie's grandmother had told Millie's mother that wise saying many years before. Millie's mother had passed the same words on to Millie. Millie hoped that, one day, she would have children of her own who would be grateful for such sound advice.

As she worked, the housemaid chirruped a cheerful song that she had heard at the music-hall, where she had gone with Cook, the week before:

> "Through the street we marched along,
> Shouting ev'ry comic song,
> Hip-hooray! Let's make hay!
> Boom diddy ay! Ta-ra-ra!"

Millie's song, accompanied by the noise of the hand-shovel on the ashes, prevented her from hearing the sound of footsteps tiptoeing across the landing.

Gerald, in dressing-gown and pyjamas, looked in at the parlour door, and then turned and signalled to his sister that it was safe to pass. Philippa, also in her dressing-gown and night-clothes, scampered across the landing and down the stairs that led to the hall and their grandfather's photographic studio. Gerald followed his sister.

Millie, unaware of what had taken place behind her back, continued to trill her happy song:

"*. . . We fairly mashed the ladies with our Oui!*
Tray Bong!"

Inside the studio, Gerald leafed through the batch of photographs that Mr Garstanton had taken the day before. It was not long before he had found the one he was looking for. He held it up for his sister to see. It was a picture of the Chinese conjuror in his oriental robes performing one of his magic tricks.

"It *was* him, Phil," said Gerald. "It was Harwell Mincing in another of his disguises." He covered the upper and lower part of the face on the photograph with his hands. "Look at those *eyes*, Phil! They're Harwell Mincing's sure enough."

Philippa studied the photograph keenly and nodded. "It's him all right. It's all our fault," she sighed. "We should have recognized him when he first arrived."

"We weren't to know, though, were we?" replied Gerald. "He caught us off-guard—what with the excitement of the party and everything."

"I wish I'd never *had* a birthday party," Philippa burst out. "That makes it all *my* fault! If I hadn't had that party,

Harwell Mincing would never have captured the little people."

"Don't be a silly goose, Philippa," said Gerald, trying to cheer his sister up. "Of course it wasn't *your* fault! In any case, we don't know for sure that he *has* got them."

But Philippa was not to be comforted. "Yes, he has," she said. "They're not here, are they? Where are they then?"

Gerald shook his head. But before he had time to think of anything to say, a voice spoke up from behind them.

"Hullo there!" It was Mr Garstanton who had walked into his studio and was surprised to find his grandchildren there. "What mischief might you two scallywags be up to?"

"None, Grandfather," said Philippa, meekly.

"We were just looking at these photographs you took at the party yesterday," put in Gerald, quickly, holding up the portrait of the Chinese conjuror. "Especially this one—isn't it good?"

"Ah! You like that one, do you?" said Mr Garstanton, pleased and flattered. He studied the photograph himself. "D'y'know, I do believe you're right. It is an excellent portrait." He tugged at his side-whiskers and pondered. "I might even enter it for the competition in this month's issue of the *Photographic Camera Magazine* . . ."

Mr Garstanton took the photograph out of Philippa's hands. He picked up another one of which he was particularly proud. It was a picture of Cook stirring a pan of soup on the kitchen range. Holding one in each hand, he studied them both in turn, first at arm's length and then up close to his face, undecided which of the two he liked the best. "I *was* thinking of entering this one for the competition," he said, nodding at the photograph of Cook. "Which one do *you* think?"

But when he turned to where the children had been standing a moment before, he found that they had slipped quietly out of the room.

"Well, I'm blessed!" murmured Mr Garstanton.

Gerald and Philippa, racing upstairs, met Millie coming downstairs from the parlour carrying a bucketful of ashes.

"You two won't 'alf cop it," she said, looking at their night-clothes. "Cook's down in the kitchen this very minute, a-boiling up that 'addock for breakfast, an' you two ain't even dressed yet!"

And she continued on her way, "tut-tutting", into the hall where she pulled the morning paper out of the door-flap.

At that moment, the old photographer came out of his studio, still puzzling over which of the two photographs he should enter for the magazine competition.

"Ah! Millie! Just the person—give me an opinion." And he held the photographs under the housemaid's nose. "Which do *you* think is the best?"

"Lawks, sir!" gulped Millie. "I don't know nuffink abaht photographicals! Don't arst me ter choose!"

"But I *am* asking you. I'm entering one of these two in a competition—the thing is, which one?"

Millie screwed up her eyes, pursed her lips and looked at the photographs in turn. First the study of the Chinese conjuror doing a trick, and next the one of Cook, stirring soup.

Mr Garstanton held his breath.

"Well, sir," Millie said at last, "if you *really* wants to know what I think . . ."

"I do! I do! Indeed, I do!"

"The truth of it is, sir, I ain't all that struck on people in a photograph, sir—I'm much more partial to a view."

"A view?" said Mr Garstanton, bleakly.

"Yeh—y'know, sir—Southend Pier when the tide's in. 'Ampstead 'eath when the sun's out, sort o' thing."

And, having given him her opinion, Millie smiled and bobbed another quick curtsy. "I'll get these ashes outside and into the dustbin, sir . . . Ooooh, an' 'ere's y'r paper, sir," she added, slipping the copy of *The Times* under his arm before scuttling down the stairs that led to the basement.

Mr Garstanton gazed, glumly, at the two photographs he was holding, one in each hand. "Southend Pier?" he murmured. "Hampstead Heath?" And, shaking his head in confusion, he set off towards the dining room.

Upstairs, in the nursery, the children were still trying to work out what might have become of their little friends, the Lilliputians.

"Supposing," said Gerald, "Harwell Mincing *tried* to catch them yesterday—but they managed to escape."

"What makes you think that might have happened?" Philippa asked, frowning.

"They have outwitted him before, Phil—they are much cleverer than he is."

"But even if they *had* escaped from Harwell Mincing, *we* still wouldn't know where to look for them. And *they* wouldn't know how to find their way back here."

"Perhaps some other grown-ups might find them. Perhaps they might look after them."

"Some hopes!" snorted Philippa. "If *any* grown-ups got hold of them, they'd put them in a zoo or something. You know what grown-ups are like!"

"But if that happened, Phil, it would be sure to be in all

52

the newspapers. At least we'd know that they were alive and well. At least we could go and try and rescue them. You never know—there might even be something in Grandfather's copy of *The Times* this morning. Let's see if we can find out anything during breakfast. Come *on*!"

But Philippa did not even seem to be listening. She was staring down, out of the nursery window, into the street below.

Victoria Street was beginning to bustle with life. A fruiterer's horse and cart was rattling along the cobblestones while the milkman's pony and trap went past it in the opposite direction. A stray dog, teeth bared, was growling at a ginger tom-cat crouched in a shop doorway, its back arched, its claws spread, purring angrily. Two workmen were striding out on their way to a factory, their black heavy-studded boots echoing along the pavement.

Philippa shivered as she considered what small chance the Lilliputians would stand in the outdoor world of studded boots, iron-bound cart-wheels, animal teeth and needle-sharp claws.

5

Harwell Mincing lashed, frenziedly, at the undergrowth with a stout stick. At the same time, under his breath, he cursed the little people, the van-man and his own bad luck.

He had come into Holdsworth Park to look for the Lilliputians at daybreak that morning. He had met with no success.

His sister, Sarah, who had accompanied him, was standing on a concrete path, at a safe distance, watching Harwell as he struck out at the long grass.

"If anyone in authority sees you, brother, they will have you taken into custody for sure," she observed, adding, "Not that that might not be the happiest circumstance for all concerned, yourself not least."

Harwell glanced around, furtively, to make sure that he was not being watched. But it was still quite early and no one else appeared to be about.

"They were mine, Sarah," he said, bitterly. "Those cunning creatures were mine for the taking. Last night, I held that pagoda in these hands with them inside it, I can swear to that!"

"Aye, Harwell," said Sarah, wearily, for she had heard similar stories from her brother all too many times before. "Last night they were real and now they're gone—like all dreams they have gone with daybreak."

Harwell chose to ignore this last remark of Sarah's. Having spent his anger on the undergrowth, he threw the stick away and joined his sister on the path. As they walked on together through the park, Harwell's eyes roamed around the lawns and flowerbeds on either side of the footpath.

"It's the truth, Sarah. That accursed van-man, devil plague him, allowed some common sneak-thief to make off through the streets with my pagoda, little folk and all!"

"The *streets*, you say?" said Sarah, shooting her brother a sharp glance. "Is that why I was dragged from my bed at this ungodly hour and made to scour the *park* with you?"

"We searched the streets half the night—and then came upon some drunken tramp—cowering in a doorway and babbling on about visitations and the curse of drink and little people. *Little people*, sister, those were his very words! He took them for an affliction and he told me that he'd suffered it in this park. He saw them here! Isn't that proof for you that at least they exist?"

"Nay, Harwell," Sarah replied with a firm shake of her head. "I shall need more than the word of some drink-besotted vagrant before *I'm* convinced."

"But they *are* here, Sarah! They are in this park still—I'm sure of it!"

"And supposing that they are? Must we needs search for a needle in a haystack?" As she spoke, Sarah waved a long thin hand to take in the acreage of lawns and flowerbeds and shrubberies that went to make up Holdsworth Park. "What chance do you stand of finding your fairy-folk in this expanse?" she scoffed.

"How many times must I tell you, sister, that they are not fairy-folk!" Harwell spoke impatiently. It was a sore point with him that he could not convince Sarah the little folk were real people. "They are human beings, sister! As real—as tangible—as you or I! And I'll get my hands on them before this day is out and prove it to you if it—"

Harwell broke off as he spotted something across the park. A gleam came into his eyes.

"It's there!" he shouted, triumphantly. "It's over there!"

With which, he plunged off across a neatly tended bed of nasturtiums, heedless of where he plunged his boots.

Across the park, a portly uniformed park-keeper, who had just arrived on duty, frowned severely as he watched Harwell's progress.

But Harwell Mincing was not concerned about park-keepers or anyone else, for that matter. He had reached the base of the statue of Josiah Holdsworth. He was gloating over the red-and-gold pagoda.

"Hmmmppphh," sniffed Sarah, dismissively, as she joined her brother. She had taken a more roundabout and law-abiding route to the statue, avoiding the flowerbeds and skirting the lawns marked *Keep off the grass*. "That's been there ever since last night," she said, looking down at the pagoda. "You don't imagine, surely, that these fairy-folk of yours are still inside it?"

"Nay, sister," said Harwell, with a crafty smile. "I give them credit for far more native cunning than that."

"They must be miles away by now."

"No, Sarah, they are only that tall, remember," and, as she spoke, Harwell measured a distance of some fifteen centimetres with his hands. "This park to them is like some vast, alien continent. How far do you think they could travel across it in the dark, on foot? I tell you, sister, you could measure their progress since last night in yards!" He smiled his crafty smile again and tapped the side of his nose with his forefinger. "I have their scent, sister—and I'll flush them out. And once they break for cover across these lawns, they're as good as in my grasp—"

Harwell did not finish the sentence. His mouth had dropped open in anger and astonishment.

Beyond the statue, not thirty paces from where the Mincings were standing, a man had emerged from behind some rhododendron bushes and was tiptoeing across the grass. The man, who was wearing spectacles and had a bald head, carried a butterfly net in one hand and a glass specimen jar in the other. He was peering down at the ground.

"The impertinent jackanapes," growled Harwell. "He's after *my* little creatures!"

At that very moment, the man swooped with his net and caught something. Harwell and Sarah watched as the man transferred his catch to the specimen jar.

"Stop, sir!" shouted Harwell, setting off again across a flowerbed. "Stop. I say! That's *my* quarry!"

The portly park-keeper who had watched, disapprovingly, the last time Harwell had trodden on the flowers, was studying him from across the park again, more disapprovingly than before.

Harwell pulled up in front of the bald-headed man as he was screwing down the lid on his jar.

"I'll thank you to hand that over to me, sir!" snapped Harwell.

"I shall do no such thing, sir!" replied the man.

"But it *belongs* to me!" howled Harwell, convinced that the jar contained one of the little people.

"By what right, sir, is it *your* property?"

"Why—by the right of ownership," blustered Harwell. "It's mine—I've been pursuing him all night."

"You've been pursuing the orange-tip butterfly in the *dark*?" exclaimed the man whose name was Seymour Rollinson and who was, in fact, a professor of Natural History at the local university.

"A . . . a what?" mumbled Harwell.

"An orange-tip butterfly," the professor said again. "An *anthocaris cardamines* to give it its proper name. And if you tell me you've been chasing them at night then you are either a liar, sir, or a bigger fool than you look!"

Harwell, lost for words, snatched the specimen jar from the professor's hands. He peered at the contents. There was indeed a butterfly inside. There was nothing, certainly, that resembled a little human being.

Harwell Mincing blinked twice and swallowed, hard. "My mistake," he muttered, handing back the specimen jar.

Sarah Mincing, who had walked across to join her brother and was standing just behind his shoulder, shook her head and raised her eyes towards heaven. There were times when she had doubts about Harwell's sanity. This was one of them.

Back at the base of Josiah Holdsworth's statue, three little figures had crept out of the pagoda and were peeping round the edge of it towards where Harwell and Sarah Mincing stood.

Sarah had been wrong. The little people *had* spent all night in the pagoda. They had gone back to it after their encounter with the tramp. Exhausted by the previous evening's adventures, they had slept soundly until they had been awakened by the sound of the Mincings' voices.

They were worried now about what to do next.

"You wouldn't listen to me, would you?" said Spelbush, rounding on Fistram. "I *said* we should have pushed on last night instead of turning back."

"In the *dark*?" retorted Fistram. "After all that happened to us? Wasn't even one misadventure enough for you?"

"It was enough for *me*!" said Brelca, joining in the argument. "Just look at this dress! I rolled right down a filthy tramp in it! *Ugh!*" she went on, shivering at the memory. "That was all *your* fault, Fistram. It was your idea to climb that tramp—I said we should have gone round him. Of all the empty-headed schemes—"

"Better an empty head than an empty stomach, Brelca," Fistram said, interrupting her. "And that's what I'm suffering from right now—I don't suppose that either of you has got anything to eat, by any chance, I'm fam—"

"*No!*" replied Brelca and Spelbush together.

"There's no need to shout," said Fistram. "I only asked a question."

"Food, food, food," snapped Brelca, "that's all you ever think about!"

"Frills and furbelows, frills and furbelows," retorted Fristram. "The only thing that ever occupies *your* mind is what you're going to wear!"

They stuck their tongues out at each other.

"Stop behaving like children, both of you," ordered Spelbush. "Give some thought to how we can escape from here."

"We can't," said Fistram, flatly. Whenever things went badly for the Lilliputians, it was always Fistram who was first to give up hope. "We couldn't move an inch across

59

that grass in daylight without being spotted. We might as well surrender now."

But Brelca did not intend to give up all that easily. "We might just make it across to those flowers," she said, pointing towards the nasturtium bed through which Harwell had trampled. "We could stop for breath halfway behind that *Keep off the grass* sign."

"We might make it," agreed Spelbush, "provided the Mincings don't look in this direction."

"It's worth a try," said Brelca. "Anything's better than standing here waiting for *those* two to come back."

"She's right," said Spelbush.

"And suppose we *do* get to that flowerbed," said Fistram, doubtfully. "What then?"

"We'll worry about that when we get there," said Spelbush. "One at a time across the grass—when I give the word. Brelca, you go first." Then, keeping one eye on the Mincings to make sure that their attentions were elsewhere, he tapped Brelca on the shoulder.

"*Go!*" said Spelbush.

Brelca set off, at a run, across the well-trimmed lawn. She paused behind the cover of the *Keep off the grass* sign, long enough to regain her breath, and then she completed her run.

"*Go!*" said Spelbush for a second time.

Fistram ran out from the shelter of the pagoda. Seconds later, he was standing with Brelca in the nasturtium stalks. Once there, he waved across at Spelbush who also made the safety of the flowerbed unobserved. The three little people exchanged grins.

"So far, so good," said Spelbush.

All this while, the Mincings had been too busy to notice

what was going on. Harwell was haggling with the professor, trying to buy the butterfly net and specimen jar from him.

"Certainly not," said the professor, in answer to Harwell's latest offer. "It wouldn't be worth my while—I'd lose half the morning going back to the university for replacements."

"Very well then," said Harwell, scowling as he rummaged around in his purse. "Five shillings—and not a farthing more!"

"Done!" said the professor, delighted at the bargain he had struck.

The butterfly net, the specimen jar and the money changed hands.

Harwell passed the jar to Sarah but kept the butterfly net himself. He gave a few trial swings and found that it fitted nicely into his grasp. He was, he felt, now well equipped to go hunting little creatures. All that was required now was a first glimpse of the quarry . . .

He did not know, of course, that the Lilliputians were watching him, at that very moment, through the jungle of nasturtium stalks in the nearby flowerbed.

"Well?" said Fistram, unhappily. "We're here. What next?"

Spelbush shook his head. He had to admit that he had run out of ideas. They were safe enough for the time being, but if the Mincings got around to looking in the flowerbed, the game would be up.

And, sure enough, Harwell had already begun his search, eyes down and butterfly net at the ready, around the area close to the statue. Sarah followed close behind her brother, specimen jar in hand. The route the Mincings were taking gave the little people more cause for concern—they were heading straight towards the flowerbed.

Gerald and Philippa were passing each other anxious glances across the breakfast table. They were eager to learn whether or not there was anything in the morning paper about their friends, the Lilliputians.

But Mr Garstanton was hidden behind *The Times* and neither of the children cared to interrupt him while he was reading.

"Well I never!" mumbled Mr Garstanton to himself, and, "Goodness me!"

Both of the children wondered whether their grandfather's muttered comments might have been caused by his reading about the discovery of some Lilliputians. There was only one way to find out.

"Ask him, Gerald!" whispered Philippa, urgently, across the table.

"I can't—not yet," Gerald whispered back. "You know how he hates to be disturbed."

Millie had just come into the dining room to clear away the dirty dishes. She was frowning at the unfinished breakfast on Gerald's plate. "Surely you ain't a-going to leave that lovely bit of poached 'addick, Master Gerald?"

"I'm not hungry, Millie."

"An' what abaht you, Miss Philippa? Ain't you a-going to leave a clean plate neither?"

"I'm not hungry either, Millie."

"Thank 'eavens the next-door's tom-cat ain't off 'is digestibles then, that's what I sez—or else that there dustbin would be in for a rare old treat!" With which, she swept away their plates and began to load the dumb-waiter.

"Bless my soul!" mumbled Mr Garstanton from behind his newspaper.

Philippa, in an attempt to get her brother to say something to their grandfather, kicked Gerald's ankle under the table.

"*Ouch!*"

Gerald had cried out so loudly that even Mr Garstanton was disturbed. "Did someone speak?" he asked, lowering *The Times* and peering over his spectacles, enquiringly, at his grandchildren.

"We were just wondering if there was anything interesting in your newspaper this morning, Grandfather?" said Gerald.

"Anything very *exciting*?" added Philippa.

But Mr Garstanton shook his head. "Nothing out of the ordinary," he replied. "The war's still battling on in South Africa—and there looks like being more trouble with these Boxer johnnies in China, but that's been going on for weeks."

"Is that all?" asked Gerald, disappointed.

"Is everything happening far away?" asked Philippa, equally downcast. "Hasn't anything happened here?"

"No," said Mr Garstanton, puzzled. "What sort of exciting things do you expect to happen round these parts?"

"We were wondering," began Philippa, "if anybody might have found somebody small—*Ouch!*"

It had been Gerald's turn to kick Philippa under the table. If she wasn't careful, his sister would give *everything* away about the little people.

"We were wondering," Philippa began again, and this

time she chose her words carefully, "if anybody might have found *anything* small?"

"What? Like a lost diamond ring, or a dropped wallet, or a missing budgerigar, d'y'mean?" asked Mr Garstanton with a frown. He shook his head again. "There's nothing turned up that I'm aware of—but then, I don't study the *Lost and Found* columns."

Mr Garstanton sighed.

There were times when he didn't understand his grandchildren at all. Why, he wondered, should they be interested in lost rings or dropped wallets or even missing budgerigars? And why, for another thing, did they spend so much time these days upstairs in the nursery? And what did they know, if anything, about the bits of food that Cook said kept disappearing from the larder? Such as little slices of Madeira cake and whole sausage-rolls and even large spoonfuls scooped out of the pink blancmange? Millie was inclined to put these odd disappearances down to mice— but surely mice weren't partial to pink blancmange, or any other colour of blancmange for that matter?

Mr Garstanton dismissed all of these questions from his mind as he took his watch out of his waistcoat pocket. "Good Lord!" he gulped as he glanced at the face. "Is it that time already? I've got a client arriving for a studio portrait sitting in five minutes time!" Then, tucking his newspaper under his arm, he rose from the table and strode out of the dining room.

Millie, who had been clearing away the breakfast things all this time, grinned at the children, mischievously. "I knows of something as 'as been lost and not been found," she said.

"What's that, Millie?" exclaimed Gerald and Philippa

64

together as they exchanged a horrified glance—what did Millie know about the Lilliputians, they wondered.

"Your appetites!" said the housemaid, gleefully, as she tugged on the rope that sent the dumb-waiter racing down to the kitchen.

Millie scuttled from the room.

"At least we know they haven't been caught yet," said Gerald.

"Unless Harwell Mincing's got them," replied Philippa, gloomily.

"We could go out and look for them ourselves," suggested Gerald.

"But *where* would we look?" demanded Philippa. "We wouldn't even know where to *begin!*"

And Gerald could do nothing more than nod his head in agreement.

Harwell and Sarah Mincing, butterfly net and specimen jar both held at the ready, were getting closer and closer to the bed of nasturtiums in their search for the little people. They did not seem to mind the occasional odd glance they were getting from the passers-by.

Although it was still quite early in the morning, the sun was well up in the sky and Holdsworth Park was already a popular visiting-place for local folk.

A little girl, about three years old, held a tight grip on her mother's hand as they made their way towards the ducks and swans on the lake.

A nanny, looking neat and capable in her blue starched uniform was pushing her charge, a baby boy, in a wickerwork perambulator.

A soldier, smartly turned out in his khaki uniform, his

brass buttons gleaming, had just walked in through the park gates.

Several other people too were ambling along the paths or relaxing on the green-painted wooden benches.

Everyone, it seemed, was enjoying the crisp clean morning air and the bright rays of the sun.

Everyone, that is, except the three Lilliputians who were still in the nasturtiums, watching fearfully as the Mincings drew closer to their hiding-place.

"I *said* we should have pushed on last night," repeated Fistram for the umpteenth time. "We should have carried on with a forced long march."

"Instead of the short tramp you forced us to go up?" asked Brelca, a trifle ruefully but still managing to make a joke about their unfortunate predicament.

Before Fistram could think of a suitable reply, however, Spelbush waved across at them through the forest of flower-stalks.

"This way!" he cried, and, "over here!"

While his two companions had been talking, Spelbush had pushed and thrust his way through the nasturtium jungle, across the flowerbed, to the other side which was bordered by a concrete path.

"Come quickly!" he urged at them again.

Brelca and Fistram forced their way through the stalks and waist-high weeds to where Spelbush waited for them.

"Look there," he said, pointing across the path.

They looked. The first thing that caught their glance were two pairs of feet standing on the path. The first pair were encased in shiny black boots above which were neatly rolled soldier's puttees. The other two feet, which were plainly female, were inside a pair of neat black lace-up brogues. The hem of the dress above the shoes was blue and starched and had been smoothly ironed.

Close to these two pairs of feet which were standing still while their owners chatted, were the four wheels and the iron frame of the wickerwork perambulator.

It was, in fact, to this iron undercarriage that Spelbush was now pointing.

"There's our escape route," he said. "All aboard!" Glancing back over their shoulders, the Lilliputians could already see the flowerbed being trampled as Harwell Mincing began his thorough search.

There was not a moment to lose.

"What are you waiting for?" snapped Spelbush to his two companions. *"Run!"*

Fistram and Brelca scampered out across the concrete path, unnoticed, and scrambled up underneath the wickerwork basket on to the baby-carriage's iron frame.

Spelbush followed a step behind them.

6

"I couldn't get out last night, Albert," said the nanny in the blue starched dress to the khaki-uniformed soldier. "I couldn't—*honest!*" she added, firmly, and as she spoke she gently rocked with one hand the perambulator that contained the sleeping baby.

"I report back to my regiment tomorrow," said the soldier, sadly.

The two of them had met beside the nasturtiums in the park at least a dozen times before. They were too intent on gazing into each other's eyes to have noticed the three tiny figures who had dashed out from the flowerbed and were now safely hidden on the iron frame of the perambulator.

"I *tried*, Albert," said the girl. "I tried ever so hard to beg an hour off last night, but she wouldn't hear of it."

"I reckon we'll sail for South Africa within the week— Gawd only knows how long that'll mean before the next time I'll see you." A frown crossed the soldier's brow as he spoke.

"You'll see me tonight though, Albert, won't you?" The nanny spoke with patient persuasiveness. She nodded down at the sleeping child. "As soon as I've put him down, I'll nip out through the back door and meet you at the end of the street. Half past seven."

"Do you swear you'll be there, Florrie?"

"I'll *be* there, Albert! I've said so, haven't I? You wait for me. I can't stop now. I'm not supposed to have come as far as the park—" She broke off and looked around, anxiously, before continuing, "I *will*, Albert. I promise you, I'll be there!"

The soldier looked hard into the girl's eyes seeking reassurance and, seeming to find it there, walked off along the path.

The nanny moved away in the opposite direction, pushing the perambulator, quite unaware that she was now carrying three extra passengers.

Harwell Mincing, still thrashing around in the flowerbed, did not even glance up as the nanny and the pram went past, moving in the direction of the park lake. Neither did his sister display any interest in the girl pushing the perambulator. Sarah Mincing was too concerned at her brother's antics in the flowerbed to bother herself with nannies and baby-carriages.

"How long must this madness continue, brother?" she snapped as Harwell trampled around in the nasturtiums.

"Until I get my hands upon the creatures, Sarah," snarled Harwell, probing with the butterfly net. "They are not far away from here, believe me—I have a nose for them."

"No, brother," sighed Sarah under her breath, "and you are not far from the mad-house either!"

By which time, the three little people, on board the perambulator's iron frame, had arrived at the lakeside. Then, as the nanny paused for a moment to watch a little girl toss bread to the ducks, the Lilliputians lowered themselves down on to the path.

Spelbush placed a warning finger on his lips and

motioned at his two companions to follow him. He led the way as the three of them scuttled, unnoticed again, out from under the perambulator and underneath the park bench where the mother of the little girl was sitting. Behind the park bench was the safe cover of a thick clump of bushes.

As the nanny moved off again with the baby-carriage, the little girl scampered back across the path and flung her arms around her mother's dress.

"More, Mama! More!" she cried, excitedly. "Ducks want more bread!"

"You mustn't give it to them all at once, Adelaide!" said the child's mother, reprovingly. She peered into a paper bag that she was holding and took out some bits of cake. "One piece at a time and make it last!"

The little girl snatched the cake out of her mother's hands. She ran back to the edge of the lake where several ducks had come out of the water and were waddling in anxious circles, quacking in anticipation of the titbits to come.

"Here, duck! Here, duck!" cried Adelaide, tossing her bits of cake on to the ground.

The ducks quacked all the more and shoved one another aside with their wings in their efforts to gobble up the crumbs.

Suddenly, to the child's surprise, a tiny figure scurried across the path and grabbed a piece of currant cake from under the open beak of an approaching angry mallard.

"Quaa—*aAACCK!*" squawked the duck.

But the Lilliputian held on tightly to his prize, refusing to give it up. It was, of course, Fistram. He paused for a moment to gaze up into the little girl's delighted face.

"Hello, man!" said Adelaide politely, in no way surprised to meet a person no higher than her knee.

"Hello, child," said Fistram, gravely returning the greeting.

Then, as the duck gave chase, Fistram turned on his heel and sped across the path back into the clump of bushes.

"Your stomach, Fistram," growled Spelbush, confronting his companion, "will be the death of all of us!"

Fistram shrugged. He sat down on a discarded matchbox, broke off a piece of the cake and held it out to Spelbush.

"Have some?" said Fistram.

"No, thank you," replied Spelbush, airily.

"Suit yourself," said Fistram. He nibbled at the cake himself. "It isn't at all bad, you know," he continued, after he had swallowed the mouthful. "It isn't stale—*and* it's got currants in it."

"I said 'no, thank you'," said Spelbush. But he had to admit to himself that the currant cake *did* look rather tempting. And he *was* hungry. "Oh, very well then," he said, grudgingly. "But only to please you, Fistram."

Spelbush took a piece of the cake from Fistram, bit off a mouthful and chewed it slowly, trying to look as if he wasn't enjoying it in the least.

"How about you?" said Fistram, turning to Brelca who was standing on guard near the entrance to the bushes. "Care for a piece?"

"I don't think there's time just now," she said, shaking her head and pointing back the way they had come.

Looking back, Fistram and Spelbush saw that the Mincings had stopped searching in the nasturtiums and were now heading straight for the clump of bushes.

71

"We need another hiding-place—and soon!" said Spel-bush.

"How about that?" said Fistram, nodding in another direction.

Spelbush and Brelca followed Fistram's glance.

Not far away, in the middle of a large circular area of concrete where several paths converged, a man was setting down a wooden box. The box was about the size of an orange crate and had a hand-hold at either end to make it easier to carry. The holes were just large enough for a Lilliputian to wriggle through.

The man, who was dressed in the uniform of a Salvation Army officer, was placing the box, which served as a platform, in readiness for a prayer meeting that was about to take place.

"That's just right!" said Brelca, excitedly. "They'll never think of looking inside there for us!"

"Provided we can get into it without being seen," said Spelbush, doubtfully.

"There's only one way to find out," said Brelca, "and that's to *try*!"

"She's right, you know," said Fistram. "If we stay where we are now, we haven't a chance."

Spelbush glanced around, quickly, and in all directions. The Mincings were still some distance away, but drawing closer every second. The little girl and her mother were busy talking. The Salvation Army officer was walking off, his back to the bushes. There was no one else about.

"Very well," said Spelbush, arriving at a decision. "And the sooner the better—let's go!"

The three little people ran out from the cover of the bushes and into the centre of the concrete circle. They wriggled, one by one in quick succession, through the nearest hand-hold in the box.

Once inside, Spelbush and Brelca smiled at each other in happy relief.

"Safe at last!" announced Brelca.

"I wouldn't be too sure," said Fistram, frowning. "Haven't you noticed anything?"

"No," said Brelca.

"Noticed what?" said Spelbush.

"This box hasn't got a bottom to it. If that man comes back again and picks it up, we're done for—we'll be spotted straight away!"

Spelbush and Brelca glanced down at their feet. Fistram was right. They were standing on the concrete.

"Oh, well," said Spelbush, shrugging helplessly. "There's nothing we can do about it now . . ."

Over by the lake, the little girl was pleading with her mother for more titbits for the ducks.

"*Please*, Mama!"

"I'm afraid there's nothing left," said the mother, showing her daughter the empty paper bag. "I *did* tell you, Adelaide, dear, to make it last. Ducks are very greedy creatures—next time you mustn't give it to them all at once."

"It wasn't *just* the ducks that ate the cake, Mama," said the little girl. "The little man came out and took some."

"Which little man?"

"The tiny one that lives in the bushes—he's only so big," said the little girl, putting her hands about twenty centimetres from the ground.

Her mother shook her head and smiled, disbelievingly. There were times when she quite despaired of Adelaide.

Little man indeed! In the bushes! The things the child made up! But then, she told herself, didn't *all* small children enjoy the world of make-believe?

But Harwell Mincing, who had overheard the child's remark, narrowed his eyes. He had arrived at the clump of bushes by the lake and was thrashing his stick around inside them.

A military-looking man, with a bristly moustache and a ramrod-straight back, who happened to be passing, pursed his lips and frowned at Harwell's curious behaviour.

"Is it not time, brother, that you forswore this madcap venture—if only for today?" suggested Sarah, who was standing near the bushes and had noted the soldier-like man's disapproval.

"Nay, Sarah," growled Harwell, beating even harder with his stick. "Not when I'm so close to the devilish little creatures."

"But the park is filling up," argued his sister. "Make a spectacle of yourself by all means, Harwell, if such is your desire—but not in my company."

"Did you not hear what that child said, sister? She *saw* a little man come out of these very bushes! I tell you, there's a fortune close at hand for both of us!"

Just then, there was the sound of music striking up nearby. Harwell and Sarah glanced to where the sound was coming from.

A Salvation Army band had assembled and was standing in a circle around the wooden box. The bandsmen and women had laid their instrument cases on the ground beside them while they played, and sang, a rousing Salvationist hymn.

As the hymn came to a spirited finish, a young lady

Salvation Army officer stepped into the centre of the circle and up on to the box beneath which were hidden the three Lilliputians.

"Our message today, brothers and sisters," she began, "is the curse of strong drink. I crave your kind attention now while our most recent convert, Mr Samuel Baxendale, tells us all about his own experiences with the demon alcohol."

As the officer stepped down from the box, a man moved into the centre of the circle.

It was the same shabby tramp who had been startled from his drunken slumbers the night before by the little people. He had managed to tidy up himself to some extent, and had even washed and shaved, but he was still instantly recognizable to the Lilliputians themselves as they peered up at him through a crack in the wooden platform.

"It's him again!" said Spelbush. "It's that tramp we scrambled up last night."

"The one you led us up, you mean," snapped Fistram.

"Ssshhh!" went Brelca, putting a finger to her lips as the tramp stepped up on to the platform. "Let's hear what he's got to say."

"Yes, brothers and sisters, one and all—I was a slave to the demon drink," began the tramp, blinking solemnly at the circle of Salvationists and bystanders. "Only yesterday, good people, I was hurtling down that well-trodden path of self-destruction to damnation! But it was in this very park, brothers and sisters, last night, only a few short hours ago, that I finally was brought face to face with the error of my ways. I suffered a visitation from the forces of the devil, friends! With these very eyes I did behold them—little folk

75

with horns and tails and countenances horrifying to look upon—"

"He surely can't mean us?" gasped Fistram.

"Ssshhh!" Brelca went again.

"—Awesome awful apparitions," continued the tramp, "with flashing eyes and fiery breath and dressed from head to foot in demon red—"

"Now that *is* going too far!" snapped Brelca. "I wouldn't be seen *dead* wearing red!"

"SssshhHHH!" It was Brelca's turn to be silenced, this time by Spelbush.

"—But from that moment, friends, I have cast strong drink aside!" The tramp paused as a ripple of applause came from his audience.

"It's that vagabond I told you of," hissed Harwell into his sister's ear. "The one I came across early this morning blubbering in a shop doorway."

The Mincings had left the bushes and moved across to stand on the fringe of the Salvation Army circle.

"—From this day forward, brothers and sisters, alcohol shall never again stain these lips!" the tramp went on, enjoying the importance of his public appearance.

"Hallelujah!" he added, and, "I thank you one and all!"

As the tramp stepped down from the platform, the young lady officer Salvationist, who had been taking a collection during his speech, approached the Mincings with her collecting bag.

"Will you contribute to the poor and needy, sir?" she said, jingling the bag of coins under Harwell's nose.

"And let the workhouses lay idle?" he snapped. "Never, miss!"

"Will you give anything, ma'am?" asked the Salvationist, turning next to Sarah.

"Certainly—I always give the poor my blessing," replied Sarah, but she made no move to open her purse.

As the lady Salvationist moved back into the centre of the circle, Harwell Mincing glanced around the area, impatiently.

"They've found themselves some cunning hiding-place somewhere near here," he growled.

"To end our meeting, brothers and sisters," began the Salvation Army lady, stepping back up on to the platform, "we shall praise the Lord and raise our voices joyfully as we sing *The Old Rugged—*"

"Box!" shouted Harwell, having had a sudden inspiration.

"*The Old Rugged Cross!*" said the Salvation Army Officer, frowning at Harwell.

"Hush, brother," muttered Sarah, aware of the curious glances they were getting from all around the circle.

"The *box*, I tell you, sister," repeated Harwell, fiercely. "They must be underneath it. It's the one place that we haven't looked and it's the ideal hidey-hole!"

Then, with all eyes turned towards him, Harwell strode into the centre of the circle and confronted the young lady Salvationist.

"I must ask you, miss, to step down for a moment," he said.

"I shall do no such thing!" replied the Salvation Army lady, stoutly. "I'm conducting a meeting here."

The bandsmen and women laid down their instruments in their cases at this interruption and looked surprised by this curious turn of events.

"It is my certain belief, young woman," said Harwell, angrily, "that there is something underneath the box on which you are standing that belongs to me! I demand that you step down from it!"

"And I am telling you again that I am staying exactly where I am!"

"In which case, miss—"

As he spoke, Harwell stepped forward to dislodge the young woman from the pedestal.

But before he was able to make a move to shift her, a hand reached out and seized Harwell by the shoulder.

"Is this the rogue in question?" asked the police constable who had taken hold of Harwell.

Harwell Mincing turned in surprise and found himself confronting both the policeman and the park-keeper who had been keeping an eye on him all morning.

"That's him, right enough," said the park-keeper. "Been misbehaving himself for hours, he has. Jumping about in the flowerbeds; ignoring *Keep off the grass* signs—and now he's pestering these good people."

"Very well then, feller-me-lad," said the constable, briskly, "I must ask you to accompany me to the police station."

"But . . . but . . . but . . ." floundered Harwell, looking anxiously around, hoping that his sister might come to his assistance.

But Sarah Mincing had had enough for one day. She had no intention of involving herself in Harwell's latest problem. Turning her head aside, she pointedly avoided her brother's pleading gaze.

"But . . . but . . ." gabbled Harwell again.

"Save your 'buts', sir, for the magistrate," said the

policeman, firmly. "Come along, quietly now—if you know what's good for you."

Harwell, realizing that he had no choice in the matter, allowed himself to be led off in the direction of the park's main gates.

The excitement over, the bystanders were moving off. The musicians were picking up the cases containing their instruments.

The lady Salvation Army officer watched Harwell disappearing along the footpath in the tight grip of the constable and with the park-keeper in attendance.

"How odd!" she observed to one of her fellow Salvationists, thinking of Harwell's strange behaviour. "What was it he was saying? Something about his owning something underneath our podium?"

Her companion stopped and lifted up the wooden box.

"Nothing under there, Eliza."

The Lilliputians had gone. They had taken advantage of the diversion created by Harwell's interference and made their escape unnoticed. They had found themselves a fresh hiding-place.

"Poor fellow," said Eliza, the Salvation Army officer, with a shake of her bonneted head. "Perhaps he's out of his mind?"

Sarah Mincing, overhearing these words from a few yards away, could do no more than sigh and nod her head in agreement to herself.

7

Gerald and Philippa were sitting at the nursery table, studying books. Gerald was managing, with some difficulty, to concentrate his thoughts on the English Civil War, but Philippa's mind was far away from the relief map of the Pennine Range in her geography book. Her eyes were red-rimmed. She had been crying most of that morning. Even now, almost twenty-four hours after the Lilliputians had disappeared, she was still having to blink back tears.

"Cheer up, Phil!" said Gerald anxiously. He was concerned both about his sister's feelings and his missing friends. "I'm sure they're all right—wherever they are. They may be small, but they *are* grown-up sailors—they sailed across *oceans* to get here, remember. They know how to take care of themselves."

But Philippa made no reply. Her brother's words gave her little comfort.

Then, through the open window, there came the sound of brass musical instruments striking up a hymn tune.

Gerald crossed to the window and looked down into the street.

A circle of black-uniformed bandsmen, bandswomen, choristers and passers-by had formed up in the street almost directly below the nursery window.

"It's the Sally Army, Philly!" said Gerald, turning to his sister, then, hoping to take her mind off things, he added, "Let's go down and join in the singing with them—you always enjoy it, Phil, you *know* you do!"

"Oh—very well, Gerald," said Philippa, but without enthusiasm. "If *you'd* like to—perhaps it will take my mind off . . ." Philippa sighed and got down from the table without finishing her sentence.

The children went out through the nursery door and down the stairs.

Outside in the street, as the music ended, Eliza, the young lady Salvation Army officer, stepped up on to the wooden pedestal and smiled round at her audience.

The Salvation Army group had walked all the way from Holdsworth Park to Victoria Street where they also regularly held their meetings. They had already been joined by several people from the houses on either side.

"Brothers and sisters," began Eliza, "we shall take our thought for today from the Book of Matthew: 'Ask, and it shall be given you; seek, and ye shall find; knock, and it shall be opened unto you!' Let us pray."

As the Salvation Army members, and the bystanders who had joined the circle, lowered their eyes to the ground, the door to the Garstanton house opened and Gerald and Philippa came out into the street. Then, as Eliza led the group in prayer, the children tiptoed quietly across and joined the circle, closing their eyes and putting their hands together, fingers pointing upwards.

"Dear Lord," said Eliza. "Let us today pray for all of those who are parted from their loved ones . . ."

But as the Salvation Army officer continued her simple prayer, Philippa quietly whispered words of her own.

"Please, *please* let the little people be safe, wherever they are," she pleaded, "and if you'll only let us find them again, God, I'll never ask you for anything again—*ever* . . ."

"Me neither," muttered Gerald who, standing close to his sister, was the only person to have overheard her words.

" . . . for ever and ever, Amen," said Eliza, bringing the prayer to an end.

"Amen," repeated the grown-ups standing in the circle.

"Amen," echoed the children.

"And now," said Eliza, brightly, "we're going to sing a hymn that we all know and love: *Onward, Christian Soldiers!*"

The bandsmen picked up their instruments again and wiped the mouthpieces with bright yellow dusters while the choristers cleared their throats.

Gerald, who had chanced to look down at the cobblestones, blinked, swallowed hard, then blinked again in astonishment.

"Look!" he managed to blurt out, nudging his sister and pointing down at the ground.

Philippa followed his glance.

Her mouth dropped open.

Her eyes opened wide.

"Golly!" she said.

Standing in the shadow of a bassoon-case stood three familiar little figures: Spelbush, Brelca and Fistram.

The Lilliputians waved up at the children, big smiles spread across their faces.

Having slipped out from under the pedestal in the park, the three little people had managed to creep, unseen, into three of the instruments before the owners had closed their cases. Spelbush had hidden inside the horn of the euphonium; Brelca had stolen inside a trumpet; Fistram had managed to slip down a trombone.

When the bandsmen had arrived in Victoria Street and set their cases down again, the Lilliputians had succeeded in stepping out again, unnoticed.

They had all three been surprised and delighted to discover that they had been delivered, safely, almost on their own doorstep. They were now equally delighted to find themselves reunited with the children.

"Onward Christian soldiers,
Marching as to war . . ."

As the band and the choristers struck up the familiar hymn, both the children and the Lilliputians, who were still standing in the shelter of the bassoon-case, joined joyfully in the rousing chorus.

It was not very long after the Lilliputians' adventure in Holdsworth Park that a curious stranger called at Mr Garstanton's photographic studio.

The man, who was tall and heavily built, had a booming voice and wore a long black coat with an astrakhan collar and a wide-brimmed dark felt hat. But the most curious thing about him was the costume he had brought along with him to be photographed in.

The children, who were peeping through a crack in the studio door, gasped in surprise as the man stepped out from behind the screen where he had been changing his clothes.

He was dressed, from head to foot, in a bright red devil's costume complete with horns and swishing tail. In one hand he carried a sharp three-pointed trident.

"Bear with me, sir," said Mr Garstanton, fussing around at the back of his camera. He was, in fact, as surprised as his grandchildren at his customer's strange choice of dress. "I'll be ready in a moment," added the old photographer, slipping a plate into the camera.

"Take as much time as you wish, sirrah," said the man, airily waving a hand in the air. " 'Twere better the deed were done well than quickly!"

"Oh, undoubtedly, sir," replied Mr Garstanton, mopping at his brow with a large spotted red handkerchief. "But I wouldn't wish to keep you in that costume any longer than was necessary—not in this heat."

It was a very hot day in late summer, on top of which there was a huge fire blazing in the studio grate.

"The heat, sir," said the visitor, giving a demoniacal smile to match his costume, "doesn't bother me in the slightest!"

With which, he threw back his head and let out deep bellowing peals of laughter that echoed round the walls of the studio.

Outside in the hall, the children exchanged puzzled glances.

"I wonder who he is?" said Philippa.

"Dunno," said Gerald. "I don't think that Grandfather knows him either—he's jolly fearsome though!"

"Perhaps he's going to a fancy dress ball?" suggested Philippa.

"Perhaps it's for a church pageant," said Gerald.

"What's that thing Grandfather's holding up now?" asked Philippa, peering again through the gap between door and door-post.

"It's his newest flash-powder gun," said Gerald, following his sister's glance. "It only came in this morning's post."

"I hope he knows how to use it," said Philippa. "You know what he's like."

"Don't I just!" said Gerald. "He might have done better to practise with it first!"

Inside the studio, the old photographer held up his very latest gadget—much improved, the leaflet said, on the old one. "In your good time, sir," he said, preparing to take the photograph.

The visitor drew himself up into a proud and devilish posture for the camera's benefit.

"Scowl, please," said Mr Garstanton—because "smile" did not seem quite the appropriate word for the occasion.

The stranger adopted a suitably fierce expression to suit his costume.

"Now!" said Mr Garstanton and, at one and the same time, he pressed his camera's exposure bulb and the trigger of the flash-gun.

"*CCcrraaAASSSHHHH!*"

There was a loud explosion accompanied by a blinding flash of light which was followed, instantly, by billowing clouds of grey-black smoke.

It was, as Philippa had pointed out, the very first time that her grandfather had used that flash-gun to light a photograph. Which was probably why he had overloaded the device with flash-powder.

The smoke cleared, leaving both the photographer and his client with blackened faces.

"Very good!" said Mr Garstanton, trying to appear as if nothing out of the ordinary had happened.

The stranger too seemed unperturbed by the experience and smiled broadly.

Out in the hall, as the dispersing smoke curled out

through the partly open door, the children reeled back, coughing and spluttering.

"That just serves you right!" said Millie, who had entered the hall from the kitchen carrying a shopping basket. " 'Ow many times 'ave you both been told about peepin' an' pryin'?" she added, gently closing the studio door.

"But there's a man in there dressed up as the devil," said Philippa.

"He's got horns and a tail and everything," added Gerald.

" 'As 'e indeed? It wouldn't come as no surprise to me then, if it wornt Ol' Nick 'imself in person neither—coming to collect the pair of you for minding other folks's business!"

"Where are you going, Millie?" asked Philippa, hastily changing the subject.

"Shopping. This 'ere h'unexpected 'eatwave ain't 'alf causing consternation in the larder. Cook's 'ad to throw out that there brisket we was going to 'ave for dinner—an' she ain't all that keen on yesterday's cold salmon neither. I'm off to the butcher's for alternatives . . ." She crossed as far as the hall door where she paused and turned. "Shopping—that's where I'm off. An' I'll tell you two scallywags where you're a-going now—upstairs. Up to that nursery. This minute. Cook's 'aving 'er afternoon nap—larst thing she needs is you pair clattering around down 'ere. Go on! You 'eard me—'op it! *Shoo!*"

Gerald and Philippa set off, slowly, up the stairs towards the bedrooms and the nursery. They stopped and turned, however, the moment that the front door closed behind Millie.

"Kitchen?" asked Philippa.

"I'll say!" replied Gerald, nodding enthusiastically. "If Cook's asleep and Millie's out, now's our chance to raid the larder for the little people's supper!"

Back in the photographic studio, Mr Garstanton was still removing soot from his face. "I hope you didn't find the magnesium flash too disconcerting?" he said.

"Not at all!" called out his client from behind the screen where he was changing back into his everyday clothes. "I never complain when I'm in the limelight—the only times I kick up a fuss are when I'm left out of it!"

"Good!" replied the photographer. "The flash-powder seemed apt, you know, for photographing Satan. It's one of those new-fangled gadgets I seldom get the opportunity to use—it tends to frighten young children and old ladies—" Mr Garstanton broke off. His visitor had just stepped out from behind the screen, resplendent again in his long black coat with its fur collar and his broad-brimmed velvet hat. A sudden thought occurred to Mr Garstanton. "Are you, by any chance, a member of the theatrical profession?" he asked.

The stranger bowed and smiled, delighted to admit to his true profession. "Allow me to introduce myself," he said, "Courtney Ellesmere, actor and tragedian!" Then, with a flourish, he handed the photographer a small rectangle of pasteboard. "My card!" he said.

"My word!" said Mr Garstanton, greatly impressed.

Gerald pulled sharply on the rope which worked the dumb-waiter, bringing it whizzing down at speed from the upper floors. Fistram, using it as a lift, was given a sudden shaking-up as the dumb-waiter braked sharply at the kitchen hatch.

"Ouch! Do you have to stop this vehicle quite so quickly!"

"Sorry," said Gerald, smiling across at Philippa.

"Where's Spelbush?" asked Fistram, as Gerald lifted him out of the dumb-waiter and carried him across to join Brelca who was standing on the kitchen table.

"Let me out of here! Let me out at once!" Spelbush's voice cried out, heatedly.

Philippa had locked the leader of the little people inside the meat-safe, temporarily, for safe keeping.

A "meat-safe" was a common piece of kitchen furniture in the days before the invention of the refrigerator. It was a wooden box, on legs, with close-mesh wire sides. It did not serve to keep food cool but it did, at least, keep the flies and bluebottles at bay while allowing the air to circulate around its contents.

"Let me out of here this second, or else there will be trouble!" cried Spelbush, rattling the wire-mesh wall of his prison and getting redder in the face as he grew angrier.

"Not until you promise to be good," said Philippa, primly. "*And* quiet," she added. "You'll wake Cook."

"It is of no consequence to me, miss, if I wake the entire neighbourhood! I am registering an official complaint and the more people that are aware of it, the better! Help! Help me!"

Spelbush stamped his feet on the wooden floor of the meat-safe and began to shout at the top of his voice.

"Oh, *do* let him out, Phil, for goodness sake," said Gerald, "before someone comes."

"If you ask me," observed Brelca, from her seat on the

88

salt cellar on the table, "he's being particularly childish—
what's he supposed to be complaining *about*?"

"He's angry because there's nothing for your supper
except water and biscuits," explained Gerald.

"What!" cried Fistram, and he too began to stamp and
shout exactly like Spelbush.

"SsshhHHH!" went Gerald, putting a warning finger to
his mouth. "Do behave, Fistram—you'll be the ones that
suffer if anyone hears you."

Philippa had now lifted Spelbush out of the meat-safe
and placed him on the table alongside his companions.
Spelbush, in better humour now that he had been released,
folded his arms and raised his eyebrows as he watched
Fistram taking his turn at stamping up and down.

"If you *should* fall into the hands of grown-ups," Philippa
pointed out, "they'll lock all three of you up inside a
museum."

"Or a zoo," said Gerald.

"Even a zoo, young man, would be infinitely superior to
the indignity of being contained inside a meat-safe," said
Spelbush.

"*Nothing* could be worse than having to exist on water
and biscuits," panted Fistram, slowing down his stamping
as he ran out of steam.

"But we've explained all that already," said Gerald.

"It's not our fault," said Philippa.

"It's the weather," said Gerald.

"It's curdled the milk."

"It's turned the butter."

"The cold salmon's gone off."

"The brisket's in the dustbin."

But all these explanations were of little consolation to the three Lilliputians who continued to glower, tightlipped, at the children.

"I suppose we *might* manage to find you a little cheese," said Philippa.

"There might even be a pot of jam," said Gerald.

The little people looked at each other, still not entirely satisfied with what was on offer.

"While Spelbush was stamping and shouting inside the meat-safe," said Brelca, "I did happen to notice behind him a cold roast chicken."

The Lilliputians and the children glanced across towards the meat-safe. Philippa had left the door ajar. True enough, inside the wooden box, there *was* a partly carved, cold roast chicken.

"I *love* roast chicken," said Brelca.

Philippa glanced enquiringly at her brother. Gerald shrugged. As far as he could see, there was no reason why the Lilliputians shouldn't have a little cold roast chicken.

Later that same afternoon, up in the nursery, Millie lifted a tray loaded with good things out of the dumb-waiter.

There were hot buttered tea-cakes; there were scones; there were pastries; there was plum cake, a jug of home-made lemonade, and other things besides.

"I knows of two someones 'oo ain't a-going to go 'ungry this partickelar tea-time!" she announced as she carried the tray across to the table where the children were seated. "Good job I managed to get to that there cakeshop afore it closed. I reckon your guardian angels must be watching over you all right. All this grand spread on top of your other bit of luck."

The children exchanged a puzzled glance.

"What bit of luck is that, Millie?" asked Gerald.

"Why? Ain't the master told you yet is-self? P'raps it's meant to be a secret. P'raps it ain't for me to speak."

"Do tell us, Millie!" pleaded Gerald.

"We won't so much as breathe a word to anyone," promised Philippa. "Cross our hearts."

"Well then," said Millie, sitting down at the nursery table and continuing conspiratorially, "that there gentleman what came to 'ave 'is photo took this afternoon in devil's clothing—would you believe, 'e's a real live play-actor no less!"

Gerald and Philippa gasped with astonishment.

Safely hidden inside the dolls' house, the Lilliputians too were hanging on Millie's every word.

"Not only that, but 'e's appearing at the 'ippodrome this very week," continued Millie. "An' not only that neither, but 'e was so taken with 'aving 'is photo took, that 'e's given your grandpa free tickets for tomorrow night's performance!"

This *was* good news!

Gerald and Philippa could not contain their excitement.

"Is it a play?" asked Philippa.

"Are we all to go?" asked Gerald.

Millie nodded her head. "It's the pantomime. About them *Babes in the Wood*, poor little mites. An' that there gentleman is the wicked Demon King 'imself!" And, having delivered herself of this momentous news as well as having laid out the tea on the nursery table, Millie got to her feet, picked up the empty tray and carried it to the nursery door where she paused for a final word. "Not only *that* neither—but they ain't for a bench like you sits on in the gods—it's an h'entire *box*! Cook and me's to go as well!" On which triumphant note, she swept from the room.

Minutes later, the children had transferred their tea to the rug in front of the fire and were trying to tempt the Lilliputians into sharing the feast with them.

But the little people, who were just finishing their own meal off the dolls' house crockery on the dolls' house table, shook their heads and turned their noses up at the invitation.

"Why not?" asked Philippa, surprised. "There's lots of things here you're all three very fond of."

"No, thank you, little girl," said Brelca. "We've already dined."

"But you didn't have very much," Gerald pointed out. "And just look at this lot! There are toasted tea-cakes, buttered scones, plum cake—"

"*And* lemonade," Philippa broke in.

But still the Lilliputians shook their heads.

"The Cheshire cheese was more than sufficient for my needs," said Spelbush.

"I had so much chicken," said Brelca, "that I couldn't face a morsel."

"My jammy sandwich has quite filled me up," said Fistram.

Even if what Spelbush and Brelca said was true, and they *had* had enough to eat, the idea of Fistram ever having had enough was hard to believe! No, there was another reason why the little people were declining the offer of more tea—and Gerald knew just what that reason was. They had been discussing the matter only moments before.

"Oh—very well then—all right," said Gerald, referring to that previous conversation, "we'll *try* and take you to the pantomime, if we possibly can—but we're not *promising* anything, are we, Philippa?"

Philippa shook her head, firmly.

But Gerald's words were enough to cheer up the little people. If Gerald said that he would *try*, they knew they could believe him. Even the mere possibility of their being included in the trip to the theatre was sufficient to raise their spirits.

It also helped, it seemed, to restore their appetites. Or the appetites of two of them, at least—for Brelca chose to stay on the sidelines as Fistram and Spelbush attacked the children's nursery tea.

For their part, Gerald and Philippa looked on, good-naturedly, as the two Lilliputians helped themselves to handfuls of plum cake and buttered scone.

8

Much later, that same night, long after both the children and the Lilliputians had gone to bed, a broad shaft of moonlight streamed in through a crack in the nursery curtains. It shone, too, through the upstairs windows of the dolls' house.

In one of the dolls' house bedrooms, Fistram and Spelbush lay fast asleep. In the second bedroom, Brelca tossed, fitfully, on her doll's wooden bed.

Outside the dolls' house, in the nursery, Philippa was also fidgeting, restlessly, in her bed. She had been awake for hours, it seemed, too excited at the prospect of the next day's theatre visit to fall asleep.

"Gerald!" she hissed at her brother's sleeping body in the bed next to her own. And, *"Gerald!"* she called again, louder this time.

"Mmmm?" Gerald struggled into wakefulness, blinking in the semi-darkness. "What is it?"

"Are you asleep?"

"Yes! What do you want?"

"Will there be a Fairy Queen?"

"Where?"

"In the pantomime, you goose!"

Gerald, fully awake now, realizing the importance that his sister placed upon the question, rolled over in his bed to face her and then gave the matter some considered thought before he ventured a reply. "I should think there's sure to be a Fairy Queen, Phil—especially as there's a Demon King."

"And will she fly?"

"I can't say for sure. She might do. She might not. Some of them do; some of them don't. But *he'll* come whizzing up out of a trap-door—with masses of red smoke and a terrific bang! It'll be really *grand*! Honestly, Phil. Now go to sleep."

"I *hope* she flies," said Philippa, earnestly. "I hope she's one that does." Then, obeying her brother's instructions, she closed her eyes and, at last, fell fast asleep.

Hours passed—or perhaps they were just minutes. The Garstanton house, with all its nooks and crannies and shadowy corners, was silent save for the steady "tick-tock" from the grandfather clock downstairs in the hall. Then there was a "whirring" sound from inside the polished walnut cabinet and the clock began to chime the midnight hour.

One . . .! Two . . .!

In his bedroom in his big brass bed with its colourful patchwork quilt, in striped nightshirt and matching night-cap, Grandfather Garstanton snored, gently.

Five . . . Six . . .!

Also in bed and fast asleep in the small back bedroom at the top of the house, Millie, her hair tied up in "rags", dreamed of a handsome soldier she had not yet met.

Eleven . . .! Twelve . . .!

And then once again the house was silent, save for the steady "tick-tock, tick-tock . . ."

Silent, that is, except for the uneasy sounds from the

95

dolls' house where Brelca was now tossing, feverishly, in her bed. The breath came out of her little body in short, fast, painful gasps.

"Brelca?" called Fistram, sitting up in bed in the next room. "*Brelca*! Are you all right? Is anything wrong?"

Then, receiving no reply, he swung his feet on to the wooden floor and tiptoed across to the plywood wall that separated the dolls' house bedrooms. In his half-awake, muddled state, he forgot himself so far as to try and open the door between the bedrooms which, like all the other dolls' house doors, was just "pretend" and only painted on.

"Brelca, what's the matter?" he called out and, in his vexation, he banged on the wall with his fists.

"What's happening?" asked Spelbush, sitting bolt up-right in bed in the room he shared with Fistram. "What's the time?"

"It's Brelca," said Fistram, unhappily. "She doesn't answer—she's been making all kinds of noises—I think she's ill."

Spelbush was out of bed immediately. "Come on," he said.

Together, they crossed to the edge of the bedroom floor. The front of the dolls' house had been left slightly ajar and they were able, by helping each other in turn, to ease themselves around the plywood wall and into Brelca's room.

They walked to the bed where, in the shaft of moonlight, they were able to make out their companion, tossing and turning and moaning, softly, in the crumpled bed-clothes.

"Brelca? Brelca—it's me, Spelbush. What's wrong?"

Brelca's eyelids fluttered open, weakly, and she stared up into the faces of her friends.

"Spelbush, I feel awful," she said, solemnly. "I mean *really* awful."

Spelbush and Fistram exchanged an anxious glance.

Not long after, when Spelbush and Fistram had managed to wake the children, Brelca and her bed were lifted out of the dolls' house, gently, and placed on the nursery table.

In the light of the nursery oil-lamp, which Gerald had turned up, they could see that Brelca's face was flushed and bathed with perspiration.

Fistram dabbed at her brow soothingly with a scrap of torn-off handkerchief.

"What do you think it is?" said Spelbush, looking up at the children.

Gerald and Philippa shook their heads. They had no idea what was wrong with Brelca.

"She needs to see a doctor," said Fistram.

"I'll be all right," said Brelca, opening her eyes again for a moment. "I'll get over it myself."

"Fistram's right," said Spelbush, firmly. "She must see a doctor."

"I'll be all right, I tell you. You *mustn't* send for a doctor—if the grown-ups find out about us, we're lost."

Spelbush shook his head. "It doesn't matter what becomes of us," he said to Gerald. "Whatever happens, she *must* see a doctor. She must have treatment."

It was Brelca's turn to shake her head, weakly, at the children. "Don't listen to him," she gasped. "I *will* get over it. I *know* I will!"

Gerald, undecided, chewed at his lower lip.

"There are all kinds of medicines in the medicine chest," said Philippa, trying to be helpful. "There's that red medicine you took, Gerald, after you'd had the measles;

and there's that green stuff Grandfather takes some-times because of his cough. And there are lots, lots more besides—and *dozens* of boxes of little pills."

"It's no good, Philippa," said Gerald, sadly. "How can we decide what to give her, when we don't know what she's got?"

Philippa thought hard before replying. "I'll find out what it is she's got," she said.

"How?" asked Gerald, puzzled.

"I'll ask someone."

"*Who?*"

"Wait and see—wait until the morning, I'll find out then."

Spelbush and Fistram exchanged a doubtful glance. They were not at all sure about Philippa's suggestion—on the other hand, there was nothing they could do before morning anyway . . .

Brelca, meanwhile, had slipped back into a fitful sleep.

The early morning sun, creeping up over the roof-tops opposite, shone through the parlour window and sparkled on the newly blackleaded grate.

Millie sat back on her knees, studied her handiwork with some satisfaction, then wrinkled her forehead as she pondered on the question that had just been put to her.

"Lawks-a-mercy, Miss Philippa," she announced at last, "I ain't no medical practitioner! What did you say they was again, them symptoms?"

"Terribly hot, Millie, and perspiring dreadfully—and an *awful* headache."

"Lumme! That don't sound too good at all, miss, do it?

And 'oo is it, may I arsk, what's suffering from this terrible h'affliction?"

"My doll—Melissa," replied Philippa, without a moment's hesitation.

"*Oh!* It's Melissa, is it?" said Millie, hiding a smile and enjoying the game. "My word, it does sound serious—we'll 'ave to get 'er back in the pink again, right quick!"

And Millie wrinkled her brow as she gave the doll's supposed illness some consideration.

Outside the parlour, on the landing, Gerald peered through the partly open door and tried to hear what Millie was saying. But it was no use. He was forced to wait until the conversation finished and his sister came out of the room to rejoin him.

"What did she say?" he asked.

Philippa let out a bewildered sigh. "What does two tablespoons of jollop mean?" she asked.

"Dunno," said Gerald.

"No," said Philippa, "and I don't think Millie knows much either."

Upstairs in the nursery, there was no improvement in the patient's condition. Indeed, if anything, Brelca seemed a little worse. Her bed had been moved back into the dolls' house, in case anyone should walk into the nursery uninvited.

Fistram and Spelbush were sitting by the sickbed, growing more anxious by the minute.

"If those children don't discover soon what it is she's suffering from," said Spelbush, "I'm insisting on a doctor."

Fistram nodded in agreement.

"No, Spelbush," murmured Brelca, weakly.

99

But Fistram and Spelbush looked determined not to take "no" for an answer.

Meanwhile, in the dining room, the children were sitting at the breakfast table, impatiently waiting for their grandfather to put down his morning newspaper.

"Grandfather," said Gerald at last, unable to wait a moment longer. "*Grandfather!*"

"Humph?" mumbled Mr Garstanton from behind his copy of *The Times*.

"If somebody was all hot and sweaty and they'd got a fearful headache—what would they be suffering from?" asked Gerald.

This time there was no reply at all from behind the newspaper.

Gerald and Philippa pulled anguished faces at each other in frustration.

"*Grandfather!*"

Mr Garstanton put down his paper, took his pocket watch out of his waistcoat, flicked it open with his thumbnail and studied the face. "A quarter past nine exactly," he said.

"We don't want to know what the time is, Grandfather," groaned Philippa.

"Don't you?" asked Mr Garstanton. "Then why on earth did you ask me?"

"We didn't," said Gerald.

"Didn't you?"

The old photographer, who could be a little absentminded on occasion, looked down at the watch that he was holding his hand, and wondered what it was doing there.

"We were talking about being ill," said Philippa.

"About somebody having something wrong with them," said Gerald.

"Something wrong with it?" Mr Garstanton put the watch to his ear, listened, shook it hard, then listened to it again. "There's nothing wrong with it at all—it's a perfect time-keeper—always has been."

"We didn't mean your *watch*, Grandfather," said Gerald, trying again. "We're talking about *illness*."

"Illness?" said Mr Garstanton, and it seemed as if the message had got through to him at last. He peered over the top of his spectacles at his grandchildren in some concern. "Is one of you reporting sick this morning?" he said.

The children sighed again and shook their heads.

"Somebody else on the sick roll then?" said the old photographer. "Cook, is it? Millie?"

"*No*, Grandfather," said Philippa, trying hard not to lose her patience. "It isn't anybody *we* know—we were talking about illness generally—"

"We were studying geography yesterday," said Gerald, breaking in, "about North India—where Father's stationed—only we read that there was a lot of sickness there."

"Oh—a desperate amount," said their grandfather, nodding his agreement. "Natives are dropping like flies except, of course, the flies *aren't* dropping, more's the pity. It's the flies that are the cause of all the trouble."

"The *flies*?" echoed the children, puzzled. "What have the flies got to do with it?"

"They carry the disease around—dysentery, cholera—all over the Asian continent. Nothing can be done about it."

"But supposing," said Philippa, "that it wasn't *in* Asia, Grandfather?"

"Supposing it was *here*," put in Gerald. "In this house."

"Ah! You're talking about Cook again? I thought she'd botched those scrambled eggs this morning. Under the weather, is she?"

"*No!* It isn't Cook at all," said Gerald. "It's just pretending. But supposing somebody *was* all hot and sticky and they'd got this awful headache, Grandfather? What would they be suffering from?"

"Hot, d'y'say? Sticky, eh?" Grandfather frowned and pulled at his side-whiskers. "Abominable headache?" The children nodded, eagerly.

"Sounds to me like something that she's eaten—must be the weather we've been having, turns everything off, y'know."

With which, Mr Garstanton disappeared again behind his *Times.*

The children exchanged a triumphant glance, slid down from their chairs and quietly left the room.

Less than a minute later, they related all that they had heard to Fistram and Spelbush.

"It must have been the chicken then," said Fistram, sitting on the edge of the dolls' house sick-room floor and swinging his legs.

"Are you sure?' asked Philippa.

"Positive."

"Fistram's right," said Spelbush, casting another anxious glance at Brelca who had drifted, again, into a deep and fretful sleep. "It *must* have been the chicken. I only ate the cheese and Fistram had a jammy sandwich. Brelca was the only one to touch the chicken."

"We know now what she's got then," said Philippa, delightedly, "chicken-pox!"

"It isn't chicken-pox, Philippa," said Gerald.

"It's food-poisoning," said Fistram.

"But she *caught* it from the chicken," said Gerald.

"Then we know what she's got and how she got it!" said Philippa.

"We know both those things, yes," said Spelbush, scratching thoughtfully at his beard. "But we still don't know how to cure her."

Fistram nodded, dolefully, in agreement.

The children's faces fell.

"Philippa?" called Gerald, peering in at the door of the parlour.

But the room was deserted and, puzzled at his sister's disappearance, Gerald continued down the stairs.

Philippa, saying that she was going to find a medical book, had left the nursery shortly after the discussion about food-poisoning.

She had not come back.

A sudden worrying thought occurred to Gerald and, hoping against hope that he was wrong, he hurried along the hall towards the kitchen. When he pushed open the kitchen door he found, to his dismay, that his worst fears were justified.

Philippa, alone in the kitchen, was sitting at the kitchen table. She had taken the cold roast chicken out of the meat-safe and, tearing slivers of meat from it with her fingers, was slowly chewing and swallowing them.

"Philippa!" gasped Gerald, horrified.

"I've got to do it, Gerald," said his sister, determinedly.

"I've got to eat some too. Don't you see—it's the only way. If Brelca's got food-poisoning, then I must get it. Then Grandfather will send for the doctor and he'll give me the medicine to cure it. I'll be able to share it with her. It *is* the only way, Gerald. Either that, or we'll have to fetch the doctor to Brelca—and then *everyone* will know about the Lilliputians. They'll take them away from us and put them on show in a museum or a zoo."

"No, Philippa," said Gerald, firmly shaking his head. "You can't—you *mustn't!*" he added, moving away.

"Where are you going?"

"To tell Grandfather what you've done. You could be very ill, Philippa. You might even . . . I have to tell him."

"*Please!* Please, don't!" begged Philippa. "If I *do* get food-poisoning, he'll be the first to know about it anyway. If I don't catch it, then there's no point in telling him. The only thing to do now, is wait and see."

Gerald took his hand off the door knob. He had to admit that Philippa was right. There was nothing anyone could do for the moment. They *could* only wait and see . . .

Scarcely an hour had passed before Philippa began to show the first symptoms of food-poisoning.

Before an hour and a half had gone by, she had been sent to bed with a fever and her temperature was steadily rising. The doctor had been called and the whole household waited anxiously.

Millie was with Philippa, sitting by her bedside, gently cooling her forehead with a damp face-cloth.

Gerald had been banished, temporarily, from the sick-room and was sitting at the bottom of the stairs, his elbows on his knees and his chin in his hands, wishing the doctor would hurry up.

Mr Garstanton was pacing up and down his photographic studio, pausing only to glance at his watch and mutter "Tut-tut!" under his breath and, "Where has the fellow got to?"

Cook was standing on the door-step, arms folded, nervously drumming her fingers, ready to usher the doctor upstairs the very moment he arrived. She let out a long sigh of relief when, at last, a hansom-cab drew up outside the house.

"Thank goodness you're here, Doctor," said Cook, taking his Gladstone bag from him.

"I'm only sorry I couldn't get here sooner," said Doctor McMurdo, following Cook into the hall. "And where is the patient?" he asked, pulling off his white gloves.

"This way, Doctor, if you please," replied Cook, showing him the stairs.

"It's all right, Cook, I'll take the doctor up to the nursery," said Mr Garstanton, who had seen the doctor's arrival through the window and had come out of his studio.

Gerald, still hunched at the bottom of the stairs, got to his feet to allow them to pass. He started to follow them up but held back as his grandfather shook his head.

"You'd better keep out of the way, my boy," said Mr Garstanton, "at least for the time being—until we know what's wrong with your sister."

"I *do* know what's wrong with her," Gerald muttered to himself, "but I'm not allowed to say anything." With which, he sat down again, miserable, at the foot of the staircase.

Inside the dolls' house, Fistram and Spelbush peered out through the bedroom window as the doctor walked into the nursery. Behind them, on the bed, Brelca was growing weaker and weaker. Everything now depended, the Lilliputians felt sure, on Philippa getting the right medicine as quickly as possible.

Mr Garstanton stood behind Doctor McMurdo watching, apprehensively, as the doctor took Philippa's pulse and then felt her perspiring forehead.

"Dear, dear, dear," said the doctor, looking down at his patient, "and what's brought this on, I wonder?"

"She comes and goes, Doctor," said Millie, who had got to her feet and now gave the doctor a quick curtsy. "She seems to be with us one minute, poor lamb, and then she's tossing and turning fit to bust as if her little life depended on it."

"And how long has she been like this?"

"It seemed to come upon her all of a sudden, Doctor," said Mr Garstanton. "She was in excellent health at breakfast time this morning, and I can vouch for that myself."

"When she *is* awake, Doctor," said Millie, "she keeps on murmuring something about food-poisoning."

"Food-poisoning?" said Doctor McMurdo, with a frown.

"*Food*-poisoning?" echoed Mr Garstanton.

"That's what she will keep a-mumbling," said Millie.

"Why?" said the doctor. "What would a child of her years know about food-poisoning?"

"And then, Doctor, she's always murmuring this name—'Brenker—Brekner', leastways, that's what it sounds like."

"Who—or what—is Brenker?" said the doctor.

Mr Garstanton shook his head and sighed, bewildered. "I haven't the faintest idea," he said. "And as for food-poisoning, it seems impossible. Cook is extremely cautious as to what she puts upon the table."

"It has yet to be established, Mr Garstanton," said the doctor rather sharply, "that it *is* food-poisoning—that's for me to diagnose."

"I wish he'd get a move on then and diagnose it!" whispered Spelbush to Fistram, in the dolls' house. Behind them, Brelca gave a little groan.

Doctor McMurdo took his stethoscope out of his Gladstone bag and began to sound Philippa's chest. "Uh-huh . . ." he mumbled to himself, and "Uh-huh . . ." he went again.

Philippa shifted in her sleep and she too gave a little groan. "Brelca . . ." she whispered. "Brelca . . . must help Brelca . . ."

"There!" said Millie. "And that's how she's been all afternoon."

Doctor McMurdo and Mr Garstanton looked puzzled.

"What do you make of it, Doctor?" asked Mr Garstanton.

The doctor shrugged, helplessly. "Frankly, Mr Garstanton, I haven't entirely reached a conclusion yet."

"But *is* it food-poisoning?" asked the photographer.

"It could be—on the other hand, there's no definite proof as yet. She's certainly showing all the symptoms of the complaint—but there are other things too. Anxiety, of some sort or another, appears to be aggravating her condition."

"Is it . . . is it *serious*, Doctor?"

"I hope not, sir," replied Doctor McMurdo. "Only time will tell us that. The most important thing at the moment is to get her temperature down—and that as speedily as possible. I could do it all the quicker though, if I knew the source of the contamination—I'd be grateful for a list of all the foodstuffs she has eaten over the past twenty-four hours."

"I can write that down for you, Doctor," said Millie.

"Good! I'm particularly interested in anything that no one else in the house has—"

The doctor broke off as Philippa's breathing quickened and she seemed to take a turn for the worse.

"Poor little mite!" said Millie.

"Mercy me," sighed Mr Garstanton.

"It *is* food-poisoning—" said a voice behind their backs. Mr Garstanton, Millie and Doctor McMurdo turned to look at Gerald who was standing by the door, a guilty expression on his face. "—and she got it from eating some chicken," he concluded.

"Are you sure of that, laddie?" asked Doctor McMurdo. Gerald nodded, firmly.

"Chicken?" said Mr Garstanton. "But we haven't had chicken—not for several days."

"Not *that* chicken?" said Millie, in some concern. "Not that chicken what's in the meat-safe? Why, that was only left there to be throwed out!"

"Let's not concern ourselves with the 'whys' and 'wherefores' now," said Mr Garstanton. "Does that information assist you, Doctor?"

"It certainly helps," said Doctor McMurdo, who had already taken out his notebook and was scribbling in it, hastily. "Are you any good at running, boy?" Gerald nodded again. "And do you happen to know the chemist's shop on the corner of Brindley Street and Fletcher Road?"

"Yes, Doctor!"

"Then take this there with all speed," said the doctor, tearing the page from the notebook and handing it to Gerald. "Tell them that I sent you, and that I require that mixture making up immediately—wait for it, and then bring it back here. Can you run all the way there and back?"

But Gerald was already halfway down the stairs.

Inside the dolls' house, Fistram was leaning over the other patient's bed. "You're going to be all right, Brelca," he whispered, reassuringly. "We're going to get you well again—there's medicine on the way."

Brelca managed a wan smile.

"All thanks to Philippa," said Spelbush.

"Yes, indeed," said Fistram. "Thanks entirely to Philippa."

That same night, although there was a chill wind cutting through the streets outside, there was a cosy fire blazing in the nursery grate and a warm glowing circle of light from the oil-lamp on the nursery table. There was also a large bottle of pink medicine on the washstand.

Philippa was now sleeping soundly.

Millie, who had volunteered to sit up with the patient, was reading a book by the light of the oil-lamp. She started as the door creaked open and Gerald, in his dressing-gown and pyjamas, peered into the room.

"What do you want, Master Gerald?" demanded the housemaid. "You ain't supposed to come in 'ere—it ain't your nursery now, you know—this 'ere's the sick-room. You're supposed to be tucked up and fast asleep in that spare bed."

"I shan't stop long, Millie," whispered Gerald, looking

down at Philippa. "How is she now?" he asked.

"Better than she was, thank 'eavens—though not as well yet as she might be."

"Is the medicine doing her good?" asked Gerald, glancing across at the dolls' house.

"That it is, Master Gerald," said Millie with a smile. "It's perkin' 'er up no end! And that's thanks to you too for fetching it so smartly!" She looked across at the window. Even though the curtains were drawn, it was plain to see that it was quite dark outside. "What time is it now?" she said.

"Almost half past nine."

"Miss Philippa," said Millie, shaking the sleeping figure, gently. Philippa opened her eyes, drowsily. "Time for your last dose of medicine afore you settles down for the night."

As Millie uncorked and poured the mixture, Gerald and Philippa exchanged a smile.

"Hullo," said Gerald.

"Hullo," said Philippa.

Philippa's eyes strayed, enquiringly, towards the dolls' house. Gerald gave her a nod, indicating that everything had been taken care of as far as Brelca was concerned.

"Straight down in one now," said Millie, proffering the tablespoonful of pink medicine. It tasted awful. Philippa pulled a face. "I know it don't *taste* no great shakes, Miss Philippa," continued Millie, "but that only goes to prove that it's doing you good."

Then, as Millie turned her back on the children, putting down the spoon and re-corking the bottle, Philippa grinned at Gerald.

"A tablespoonful of jollop," she whispered, echoing Millie's words of over twelve hours before.

"You *are* improving fast, young lady," said Millie, who had overheard.

"And as for you, Master Gerald, you can sling your 'ook afore your grandpa comes in an' catches you! Go on—you 'eard—buzz off!"

"See you tomorrow, Phil—sleep well!" said Gerald, softly.

"Goodnight," replied Philippa and, as Gerald left the nursery, she settled her head on the pillow.

"I'm blessed if I can understand it," said Millie, frowning, as she held up the medicine bottle.

"What's that, Millie?" said Philippa, opening one eye.

"Why, this stuff 'ere," said Millie. "You ain't 'ad no more than a couple of doses out of it, to my certain knowledge, and it's 'alfway down the bottle already—if I didn't know no better, Miss Philippa, I'd swear someone 'ad been 'elping themselves to it—but 'oo'd want to 'elp themselves to somebody else's nasty-tasting medicine?"

"I can't imagine, Millie," said Philippa, smiling to herself, as she glanced across at the dolls' house in the corner of the nursery.

Inside the dolls' house, where the red glow of the nursery fire lit up the bedroom, Brelca was sitting up in bed. Spelbush was giving her a Lilliputian-sized dose of the pink medicine from one of Philippa's dolls' tea-set spoons. Fistram, in a corner of the bedroom, dipped his forefinger into an inkwell full of the medicine which Gerald had managed to filch from the nursery bottle. Fistram licked the medicine off his finger and pulled a face.

"It might be the same *colour* as pink blancmange, Fistram," said Spelbush who had been watching his companion, "but that doesn't mean that it tastes the same!"

Brelca smiled. She too, like Philippa, was well on the road to recovery.

Gerald, looking downcast, was standing in the hall outside his grandfather's photographic studio. It was the day after Philippa's attack of food-poisoning and Gerald had been told, by Millie, that his grandfather wished to see him. Gerald had a sneaking feeling that the interview was not likely to be a pleasant one.

The door to the studio opened and a lady came out. She was rather chubby, wore a broad smile and, perched on her head, there was a hat that seemed to consist mostly of a dead pheasant. She was carrying a large carpet-bag.

"Good-day, Miss Entwhistle," said Mr Garstanton, who had also come out of the studio in order to escort the lady to the front door.

"Good-day to you, Mr Garstanton," said the lady, widening her smile even more, "and thank *you* for the sitting."

As the front door closed behind his customer, Mr Garstanton peered at Gerald, enquiringly, over the top of his gold-rimmed spectacles.

"Millie said that you wished to speak to me, Grandfather," said Gerald, in some trepidation.

"No, Gerald," said Mr Garstanton, leading the way into the studio. "I rather wondered whether there was anything that *you* wished to say to me?"

"Only that I'm very sorry, Grandfather."

"I'm glad to hear it."

"And that it won't happen again."

"I should hope not indeed! You not only allowed your sister to eat rancid meat—you then chose not to advise me of the fact. The consequences could have been extremely dangerous." Mr Garstanton paused. Gerald looked down at the carpet and shuffled his feet. "However, you seem to have learned your lesson—and you have already suffered some sort of punishment in having had to forgo the pantomime last night. Under the circumstances, Gerald, we'll consider the incident closed."

"Yes, Grandfather—thank you," said Gerald, moving towards the door.

"One moment! The lady who left just now is an associate of Mr Ellesmere. She is also appearing in the pantomime. By an odd coincidence, she's given me complimentary tickets for a box at next Saturday's performance. I cannot find it in my heart to punish you twice for the same thing."

A smile spread slowly across Gerald's face, then:

"Will Philippa be well enough to go?" he asked.

Mr Garston smiled too. "The difficulty, I imagine, would be in trying to dissuade her."

Gerald, overjoyed, ran from the room to pass on the good news to his sister.

There was an enormous "*Bang!*" accompanied by a cloud of thick red smoke and then the Demon King shot up through a trapdoor and on to the stage of the Hippodrome Theatre. His appearance was greeted by hisses and boos, but Courtney Ellesmere didn't mind those at all. Happily, he hissed and booed back at the audience.

But the catcalls quickly changed to cheers when the Fairy Queen made her appearance, flying in on a wire from somewhere above the stage. And if, perhaps, she was a trifle stout, causing the wire to sag in the middle, nobody seemed to notice it.

"That's *her*, Phil!" Gerald whispered. "That's the lady that Grandfather photographed—the one who gave us the tickets for this afternoon."

"Sssshhh!" went Philippa, in reply. She didn't want to know what the lady did in her private life—as far as Philippa was concerned, she was the Fairy Queen, no more no less.

"OOooooh! Ain't she *pretty*!" murmured Millie, who was sitting in the box behind the children.

"She is indeed!" Cook agreed. "If you want *my* opinion, it's a treat-and-a-half is this one!"

Mr Garstanton, who was standing at the back of the box, smiled benignly. He was glad that everyone in his party was enjoying the pantomime. He was not aware, of course, of the three extra guests who were also present.

Spelbush, Fistram and Brelca were hidden out of sight of the three grown-ups. Brelca was peeping from under Philippa's hat, which had been carefully placed on the ledge at the front of the box. Spelbush was hidden behind the programme which Gerald had propped up in front of him. Fistram was sitting in the box of chocolates, helping himself to the last orange-cream.

It was, they all agreed afterwards, one of the nicest afternoons they had ever spent!

9

Millie picked up the letters from the hall mat almost as quickly as they fell. She walked along the hall, knocked on the door of the photographic studio and went in.

"The third post's just come, sir," she said, handing the letters to Mr Garstanton.

The photographer thumbed through them and took out one that caught his interest. "Ah, good!" he said. "Here's one from the house agent—that'll be someone wanting to look over this place, I don't doubt."

A frown crossed Millie's brow. "Beggin' y'r pardon, sir—but with regard to your moving 'ome and that—I'm wonderin' whether to 'and in my notice, sir, beggin' y'r pardon . . ."

"Hand in your notice, Millie?" exploded Mr Garstanton in astonishment. "Why, I wouldn't countenance the thought! You're part of the family—we could hardly move without you."

"But I dunno as I'd take to living in the country, sir," said the housemaid, doubtfully.

"Why ever not?"

"Well, sir—it's the thought of all that grass for one thing, ain't it? An' all them h'animals too, for something else. I mean, say what you like sir, but you can't say as 'ow it ain't downright unnatural."

Mr Garstanton blew out his cheeks and shook his head. "Believe me, Millie, it's the hustle and bustle of the city that's the *unnatural* way of life," he said. "Why—I saw *two* of those infernal horseless carriages in the High Street *at the same time* yesterday!"

"Motor cars, sir?"

"Is that what they call 'em? *Two* of 'em there were, both at the same time, if you please, thundering along at seven or eight miles an hour, I shouldn't wonder! Think of the petrol fumes, if not the public danger, Millie! No, the change can't come soon enough for me. Only let me get this place off my hands first, and we'll be on our way—and you with us, I won't take any 'no's' on that count—just wait until you get a sniff of that country air!"

"But what will you *do*, sir?"

"Do?"

"Your work, sir," said Millie, waving a hand to take in the studio and all the cumbersome camera equipment it contained. "All your photographicalizing. You won't find many *h'animals* as wants their pictures took."

"Now that's just where you're wrong again. Picture-postcards!" exclaimed Mr Garstanton. "That's where the future of the camera lies. I shall make a positive fortune, Millie, taking portraits of the countryside—while you and Cook and the children will go around with roses in your cheeks . . ." The photographer paused and glanced up at the ceiling, in the direction of the nursery which was two floors above. "I'm sure you won't hear any complaints from my grandchildren about moving on," he said with a smile.

At that same moment, up in the nursery, the children had other things to think about.

Gerald and Philippa had challenged the Lilliputians to an

indoor sporting contest. They had placed the bagatelle board on the nursery carpet and Gerald had one ball left to play.

He struck the steel ball with the wooden cue and it rolled around the board and then rattled into a pocket. Adding up his score, Gerald discovered to his delight that he had made three hundred and forty.

"Beat that," he said, turning to Spelbush.

But the Lilliputian shook his head. "Not until you've told us more about this moving to the country," he said.

"We can't do it," said Fistram. "We *won't* go."

"I'm not a country kind of person," said Brelca.

"It's completely out of the question," said Spelbush.

The little people, it seemed, shared Millie's concern about exchanging town life for the countryside.

"It's not our fault," said Gerald.

"It was Grandfather's idea," said Philippa.

"But this is our home port," said Spelbush, looking around the nursery.

"We've lowered our anchor here," said Fistram.

"We've raised our colours," said Brelca.

"There have been problems enough for us here in the city," said Spelbush, sternly. "The prospects of having to survive in a giant-size rural environment are too horrendous to consider."

"Supposing we lost our way and wandered into a pig sty?" said Brelca. "We'd be up to our necks in mud!"

"What if we strayed into a meadow full of cows?" said Fistram. "One false step and we'd be up to our ears in . . ." He left the sentence unfinished.

Spelbush nodded, gravely. "I'm sorry," he said to Gerald, "but we just can't do it."

"It won't be *that* bad," replied Gerald.

"At least you'll be taking your home with you," said Philippa, glancing across at the dolls' house. "We've got to leave all this behind," she added, wistfully, looking around the nursery.

"*And* you'll be escaping from the Mincings," Gerald pointed out. "They'll never find you in the country."

"If only it could be that simple," said Spelbush, sadly.

"That pair of villains won't give up easily," said Fistram.

"They followed us here after the shipwreck," said Brelca, "they'll follow us wherever we go."

"But they won't be able to," said Gerald. "Not if they don't know where you've gone."

Spelbush shook his head. "They'll find out where we are," he said. "And if I know that pair, they're probably making plans already to pursue us." Then, as if dismissing the Mincings from his thoughts, he weighed the bagatelle ball in his hands carefully, and then bowled it down the board as if he was in a bowling alley.

As it happened, Spelbush was right. The Mincings *did* know that Mr Garstanton intended to move on. They had seen the "For Sale" sign outside the house. They had also guessed, quite rightly, that the children would want to take the Lilliputians with them. But Sarah Mincing, it seemed, had had enough of the battle of wits.

"Good riddance to them, I say, brother," she said, as she poured herself a cup of tea in the living room of their apartment. "Let them go. And good riddance too to the Garstanton brats. I shall be glad to see the back of them—and put an end at last to this wild-goose chase."

Harwell, who was holding a false moustache up in front

of his face while he examined his image in the mirror above the fireplace, frowned at his sister over his shoulder. "While I, Sarah, on the contrary," he said, "would willingly follow the little creatures to the farthest ends of the earth, if need be."

"Then you shall travel there alone, Harwell," snapped Sarah. "My mind was made up even before this latest piece of news. I'm going back to my boarding-house on the coast."

"And what will that avail you, do you think?" growled Harwell. "You rarely saw any lodgers. Shall you choose to live in poverty for ever?"

"If I must, brother, if I must," snapped Sarah, who did not like being reminded of the fact that she had never been a successful boarding-house landlady. "At least I shall live in *honest* poverty," she said, folding her hands over her apron and rubbing the back of one hand with the fingers of the other.

"Oh, I don't doubt it, sister," replied Harwell. "And with the ultimate satisfaction, too, of going to your grave an *honest* pauper."

"And what's wrong with that—if it gives me the added pleasure of going there a sane one!" Sarah Mincing still had her doubts about the existence of the little people—she had a sneaking suspicion that they dwelt only in her brother's mind. "The path that you tread, brother, leads only to the public mad-house—and you'll not drag *me* along that road with you."

"Listen to me, Sarah," said Harwell, urgently. "There is no need for us to travel farther along any path than we've come already—here's my plan—"

"Nay, Harwell," Sarah interrupted, shaking her head,

firmly. "I've already told you of my decision—I'll not change it now."

"Only *trust* me, sister," begged Harwell. "This move of the Garstanton brood presents us with the very opportunity we've sought all these months!"

"I fail to see how."

"The house is up for sale, Sarah. I've been in touch with the agent and told him that I'm interested in purchasing it."

"*You?* Purchase the Garstanton house? With what, one wonders?"

"Will you listen to me, sister!" snarled Harwell.

"Listen to a madman? No! And even if you *did* have the money to pay for it, what do you want it *for*? Do you imagine, in that fevered mind of yours, that the Garstanton house is populated, from cellar to attic, with your fairy-folk?"

"Of course I don't! And of course I don't intend to buy the place. I only wish to gain admittance to the house—which is what my plan has achieved for me. I have an appointment to view this very afternoon. Don't you realize what this means, sister? As a prospective buyer, I shall be able to search the building from top to bottom! Search it, Sarah, seek out those devilish creatures wherever they are hidden—and swoop on them!"

As he spoke, Harwell scooped up an imaginary Lilliputian with his hands.

But Sarah was not impressed.

"Whilst the pair of brats stand by and watch you do it, I suppose?" she said.

"No, sister—for while I am scouring the house for the

cunning creatures, you will be holding the attention of the Garstanton children in the parlour."

"I beg your pardon, brother?" said Sarah, in some surprise. "Did you say *I* would?"

"I did indeed! On this particular occasion, Sarah, you are to accompany me."

"But they *know* me. Both the old fool *and* his ill-mannered grandchildren. Have you forgotten? They were boarders in my seaside establishment for over a fortnight last summer. They would recognize me instantly."

"Not in the disguise that I have planned for you, sister," said Harwell, smiling a crafty smile and tapping the side of his nose with his forefinger.

"A fig for your disguises!" snapped Sarah. "What with your play-acting and your Tom-Thumb people . . . When will you learn to live in the *real* world, Harwell?"

"Trust me, sister."

"I have trusted you too many times already! And supposing I *do* go along with your scheme—what about the old fool of a photographer? If I'm to keep the children busy, who's to deal with him?"

"I'll take care of Garstanton—he's easy enough to handle. Leave him to me. I tell you, Sarah, bear with me this one last time!" Harwell spoke with such conviction and force that even Sarah was half-won over to his cause. "We cannot fail but win," he continued. "And then we shall hold that fortune in our grasp! Why, we shall dine so well and dress so elegantly, sister, that we shall be the envy of the world!"

"Vanity, vanity, Harwell," muttered Sarah, as she stirred her tea. "All is vanity!"

121

Sarah Mincing was sitting upright on the edge of a hard-backed chair in the Garstantons' parlour.

Harwell had been right for once. The disguise he had provided her with was an excellent one. She was wearing long, black widow's weeds and the black hat on her head had a thick black veil that hid her face completely.

Harwell, standing behind his sister's chair, was dressed as a Scottish missionary. He had on a vicar's dog-collar, a linen jacket and a pair of pinstripe trousers. In his hands, he nursed a prayer book. His costume, with the assistance of a false ginger beard and wig he was also wearing, were sufficient to fool Mr Garstanton.

"Thank you, Millie, that will be all," said the photographer to the housemaid who had just brought in a tray containing a decanter and some sherry glasses.

"Very good, sir," said Millie, bobbing her usual quick curtsy. She glanced, curiously, at the two visitors as she scurried out of the parlour.

"Will you take a glass of Madeira wine before you view the premises, Reverend . . . er . . . er . . ." Mr Garstanton's voice trailed away as he realized that he did not know his caller's name.

"MacDougall, sor," said Harwell, helpfully, in a broad Scots accent. "The Reverend Hamish MacDougall, sor, at y'r service. Y'll not tak offence, I trust, if I decline the offer?"

"Not at all, reverend," replied the photographer and then, smiling at the veiled Sarah, he added, "Perhaps your wife might care to partake?"

Sarah shook her head fiercely, and her veil trembled in front of her face. "Nay, sir," she replied, in an accent that was even broader than the one her brother had used. "We have preached abstinence to the heathen in the four corners of the world, d'y'ken—we believe it our solemn duty to practise what we preach."

"I quite understand," said Mr Garstanton, replacing the stopper on the decanter. "Was it Africa you said that you'd just returned from, reverend?"

"Aye, sor, it was indeed. Bechuanaland to be precise. Following in the footsteps of the great Doctor Livingstone himself. We ran a wee mission hoose on the left bank of the Zambesi."

"Very courageous of you both," said Mr Garstanton.

"The guid Lord summoned and we answered the call," said Sarah.

"I held services twice daily," said Harwell, "while my dear wife and helpmeet, Flora, played the hymn tunes on the harmonium. It was a simple but fulfilling way of life, until—" Harwell broke off and let out a long, sad sigh.

"Until what, reverend?" asked Mr Garstanton.

"Until, at last, the debacle overtook us, sor. It does'na hurt too much, dear, if I talk of it?" he said to Sarah, patting her shoulder comfortingly.

Sarah shook her head bravely and, as her brother continued, she took out a lace-edged white handkerchief and dabbed at her eyes beneath her veil.

"Until the Good Lord, in his infinite wisdom," said Harwell, glancing heavenwards, "chose to take both our wee 'uns to be up there, nearer unto Him, in Heaven."

"Your wee 'uns?" echoed Mr Garstanton, not understanding Harwell's thick Scots brogue.

"Aye, sor—our bairns, d'y'ken, were taken from us."

"Oh, I see!" said the photographer. "You lost two children in Africa?"

"A wee lad and a wee lassie," sighed Harwell.

"No!"

"Believe me, sor, it's true. Our boy, Bertram, bless him, was borne off by a band of brigands."

"How dreadful for you!"

"Aye." Harwell plunged on, unable to stop the flood of words beginning with "B" that poured out of his mouth. "We try to banish our baser instincts and beg to believe we're not bereft and that the bandits have but borrowed the bairn to bring up as their bondson."

"You bare the burden bravely," said Mr Garstanton, catching the bug himself.

Harwell paused, swallowed, and tried again. "As for our dear daughter, Dorothea," he began, and now the "D"s had taken over from the "B"s.

"Another disaster?" ventured Mr Garstanton.

"Definitely deceased," said Harwell, ploughing on again. "I dread to say it, but we detected her demise, d'y'ken, when we discovered she'd been devoured by one of the darkest jungle's deadly denizens!"

"You must have been utterly devastated!" gasped Mr Garstanton.

"We durst hardly dwell upon it these days . . ." Harwell paused to collect his thoughts. He had to stop using words that began with the same letter, he told himself. He managed it at last by talking slowly. "But you will ken, sor, why we decided to put that dark continent behind us and chose to return to our native shores."

"I do indeed."

"It is our decision, d'y'ken," said Sarah, "to open our own small Christian orphanage."

"What a worthy cause!"

"In memory of our own two dear wee 'uns," said Harwell. "Only a small establishment—within our own meagre means. I'm here to tell you, sor, that at first glance this hoose would admirably seem to suit our needs."

"Then we shall speak about it no more, reverend," said Mr Garstanton, moving towards the door. "You shall view the premises immediately. Shall Mrs MacDougall accompany us?"

Sarah shook her head again beneath her veil.

"I feel sure, sor," said Harwell, "that my dear sweet wife would rather bide where she is a wee while, provided you've no objection."

"None whatsoever, I assure you," said Mr Garstanton. Then, turning to Sarah, he added, "Pray make yourself at home, ma'am, I do beg of you."

"She is entirely devoted to the upbringing of children, sor," said Harwell. "She dotes upon the wee darlings—I'm sure you can understand—you may have once had children in the hoose yoursel'?"

"Indeed! Indeed! Why, I've two in the hoose . . ." Mr Garstanton paused and corrected himself, " . . . *house*, at this very minute—my grandson and my grand-daughter."

"Did you hear that Flora! A wee lad and a wee lassie just like our own two sadly departed bairns," said Harwell and, turning back to Mr Garstanton, he added, "Why, sir, it's almost impossible to believe that such a coincidence could happen!"

"It is a fact though. Their names are Gerald and Philippa."

"I wonder, sor," began Harwell, about to put the next part of his plan into action, "whether I might beg a favour?"

"Ask away, reverend, ask away!"

"Do you think that Flora might be allowed to meet your grandchildren the noo—it would afford her so much pleasure, d'y'ken?"

"She shall do more than that, reverend," said Mr Garstanton, enthusiastically—unwittingly falling into Harwell's trap. "They shall sit with her in this very room—they shall *read* to her, reverend, while you and I inspect the house."

"Did you hear that Flora!" cried Harwell, clapping his hands together in pretended joy. "Oh, sor, you'll not know how much pleasure you are bringing to a bereaved mother's heart!"

"Wait one moment," said Mr Garstanton.

Then, as the old photographer walked out of the parlour to summon his grandchildren down from the nursery, Harwell and Sarah exchanged a triumphant smile.

Their scheme to capture the little people was going entirely to plan.

10

The children were sitting on the rug in front of the nursery fire, playing Snakes and Ladders with the little people, when their grandfather called out to them up the stairs.

"Gerald! Philippa! *Children!* Are you there?"

As Gerald got to his feet, Philippa motioned to the Lilliputians to run back into the dolls' house.

"Hide! *Quickly!*" she said.

Spelbush, Brelca and Fistram jumped up and ran round in circles agitatedly for several seconds before setting off in the right direction.

"What is it, Grandfather?" called Gerald. He had come out on to the landing and was leaning over the banister rail.

"Come down to the parlour—both of you!"

"*Now!*"

There was a note of disappointment in Gerald's voice. He had just thrown a six and moved his counter up the longest ladder. All he needed now was to throw a five and he had won the game.

"At the double!" called back Mr Garstanton. "On parade, this instant! We've got visitors who'd like to meet you."

"I'll bet it's those people who have come to look over the house," said Philippa, as she joined her brother on the top landing.

"But why should they want to look at us?" said Gerald, with a puzzled frown.

Philippa shrugged her shoulders.

"Come along, troops!" called their grandfather, getting impatient. "Form up on the barrack square! Smartly does it now!"

"We'd better go," sighed Philippa.

"What about *you-know-who*?" whispered Gerald.

"They're all right. They're in the dolls' house—and I've hidden that away too—in case the visitors start to poke and pry in the nursery."

"Hidden it where?" hissed Gerald.

"Out of sight," Philippa whispered back at him as they set off down the stairs.

Philippa had put the dolls' house in the bottom of the toy cupboard and shut both the cupboard doors. In her haste, she had not noticed that one end of the dolls' house was balanced on a toy drum. The dolls' house was leaning at a sharp angle. It was also very dark in there with the toy-cupboard doors shut tight.

The little people, thrown off balance, had tumbled down to one end of the dolls' house living room. They now found themselves unable to stand up.

"Where are we?" asked Fistram, nervously.

"In the dolls' house," said Spelbush.

"I know that!"

"In the dark," said Brelca.

"I know that too!" snapped Fistram. "But *where* in the dark?"

"Just a moment," said Spelbush.

He took out of his pouch a candle-stub that he kept for just such emergencies. He also took out his tinder box and, in a moment, had struck a light. The candle flame sputtered and then flickered, brightly. Spelbush held the candle up and peered at the living-room floor that sloped steeply away in front of him.

"Why is the house leaning so?" asked Fistram, unhappily. "It feels as if we're on a mountainside!"

"Bring the candle over here, Spelbush," said Brelca. "Over by the window."

Spelbush scrambled along, awkwardly, by the edge of the room where the wall met the floor, struggling over or around the pieces of dolls' house furniture which had also tumbled down the slope, holding the candle in front of him. Arriving at the spot where Brelca was crouched, he lifted the flickering candle up to the window. They peered out, together, into the darkness beyond.

The face of an angry lion, mouth open and teeth bared, stared back at them from close up against the windowpane.

"Perishing plumstones!" cried Spelbush, fearfully. "We're in some sort of jungle!"

"Don't be stupid, Spelbush," snorted Brelca. "It's a *toy* lion. It belongs to the children's Noah's Ark. We're in the toy cupboard again."

"So we are," gulped Spelbush, and he let out a sigh of relief.

"I must say," grumbled Fistram, "I do object most strongly to being bundled, higgledy-piggledy, into the toy cupboard every time this household has visitors!"

Spelbush pushed out his lower lip thoughtfully. "On the other hand, Fistram," he said, "it *is* somewhat comforting to know that the children are developing *some* sense of responsibility for our predicament."

"Responsibility!" gasped Fistram, glancing round at the

129

sloping floor and the upturned furniture. "Do you put this lot down to responsibility? Do you call it responsible of them then, to shove us away like a box of dominoes or a game of tiddly-winks?"

"Oh, do stop *complaining*, Fistram," said Brelca. "Spelbush is right—it's far better to have been put away than left out on the floor for the maid to come across."

But Fistram didn't agree with his companions. "Responsibility!" he continued. "Just look at the way they've left the floor! Look at the furniture! If this is responsibility— give *me* a good old-fashioned earthquake any day of the calendar!"

Meanwhile, in the parlour on the floor below, Gerald and Philippa were sitting side by side on the sofa. They were staring nervously at the thick, black veil behind which was hidden the mean, pinched face of Sarah Mincing who sat opposite them.

"Are you *sure* that Mrs MacDougall wouldn't rather have the children read to her aloud out of one of their story books?" said Mr Garstanton, tentatively.

"Indeed, no, sor," replied Harwell. "My dear wife, like ma'sel', considers that life is far too serious to waste any time on story books. She'll derive great pleasure in taking them through their catechisms."

Gerald and Philippa pulled sorrowful faces at each other. If there was anything they hated, it was having to recite their catechisms.

"If you're sure that it's no trouble for her, reverend?" As he spoke, Mr Garstanton flashed his grandchildren a sympathetic smile—it was, after all, he told himself, *his* fault that they had been landed in this unfortunate situation.

"No trouble at all, sor," said Harwell. "Believe me, it will give her great satisfaction to perform the task."

There was nothing more the photographer could do to help his grandchildren. "Very kind of her, I'm sure," he mumbled.

"As I have already told you, she *dotes* on children," said Harwell. "Shall we get about our business then?" he added, picking up a Gladstone bag that he had brought with him, eager to get on with his search for the little people.

Mr Garstanton, after giving his grandchildren another apologetic glance and shrugging his shoulders helplessly, led Harwell out of the parlour.

Alone with Gerald and Philippa, Sarah's cold eyes narrowed behind her veil.

"Stand up then, both of you," she ordered. "If the Good Lord had intended us to sit down all day, he would not have put feet on the end of our legs, would he?"

Gerald and Philippa exchanged a despairing glance but did as they had been told.

"I'll hear your catechisms now—and I trust that you are both conversant with them," Sarah continued. Then, looking straight at Philippa, she snapped, "What is your name?"

"Philippa Florence Victoria."

Gerald forced back a giggle as his sister was made to say aloud the two middle names she hated.

"What is *your* name?"

"Gerald Ewart Laurence."

And now it was Philippa's turn to put her hand over her mouth.

"Don't fidget! Stand up straight, the pair of you, and pay attention!" Sarah paused, glared at them both from behind her veil, and then led them into their catechisms. "What did your Godfathers and Godmothers then for you?"

The children let out longsuffering sighs, in unison, and frowned as they concentrated their thoughts upon giving the required answers to the questions.

While this interrogation was going on, Mr Garstanton had begun to show Harwell Mincing over the house. They had started in the dining room.

"It seems exactly the home that I am looking for, sor," said Harwell, clasping his hands together in pretended delight. "The Hand of Divine Providence has surely reached down this day!"

"Shall we continue, reverend?" said the photographer, leading the way out of the dining room and back on to the first-floor landing. "Upstairs or downstairs next?"

"I wonder," began Harwell, glancing eagerly towards the upper floor, "would you have any objection to my continuing the inspection on my own?"

"None at all, reverend, if that is your desire."

"Oh, it is, it is! The Good Lord has directed me to this abode—I would like to spend some moments now in quiet contemplation. In His presence alone," said Harwell, in mock pious tones.

"Do so then by all means, reverend. Can I direct you first to any particular room in the house before I leave you to your thoughts?"

"That you can, sor!" said Harwell with a sudden passionate intensity, forgetting himself for the moment. "Tell me, I beg of you, where I might find the nursery!"

Mr Garstanton blinked in surprise, taken aback slightly at the depth of feeling in Harwell's words. "It's through the door immediately facing you at the top of these stairs."

These missionary-chappies, he told himself, were curious birds! Then aloud he said, "I shall be downstairs in my studio, if you should need me."

Harwell watched the photographer go down the stairs and then he crossed and put an ear to the parlour door.

"What is thy duty towards thy neighbour?" Sarah's voice could be plainly heard.

"My duty towards my neighbour," replied the children, in unison, "is to love him as myself, and to do to all men, as I would they should do unto me—"

Harwell smiled his crafty smile and rubbed his hands together in pleasurable anticipation of what was to come. There was nothing to stop him now from searching every inch of the nursery and, he felt sure, getting his hands on the cunning little creatures at long last . . .

He set off towards the upper landing, taking the stairs in leaps and bounds.

Inside the nursery, inside the toy cupboard, inside the dolls' house, Spelbush placed a forefinger to his lips.

"Ssssshhh!"

"What is it?" asked Brelca.

"I'm sure I heard footsteps on the stairs."

"What of it?" said Fistram. "What else would you expect to hear on the stairs? Someone doing handstands?"

"Stranger's footsteps," said Spelbush, and, "SsssshhHHH!" he went again.

Harwell flung open the nursery door and stood quite still for several seconds, peering all round the room.

"Where? *Where!*" he muttered to himself. "Where do those brats keep the accursed little freaks?" He tiptoed across to the table where he put down his Gladstone bag, opened it, then glanced all around the room again. "Come

133

out, my little ones!" he chirruped. "Come out, my pretties! Reveal yourselves now to your kind Uncle Harwell!"

Inside the dolls' house, the Lilliputians exchanged anxious glances as they realized who it was that had come into the nursery.

"Here's a nice warm bag for you to snuggle down in!" they heard their enemy call. And then, as he lost his temper, he added, angrily, "Show yourselves, confound you!"

Spelbush shot another warning glance at his companions, once more indicating that they were to keep still and silent, and then he blew out the candle-stub, plunging the dolls' house into darkness.

"Very well then, if you won't come to me, I must needs come to you," snarled Harwell, peering under the furniture and then behind the books along the bookshelves. "But you shall pay dearly for the inconvenience when I do lay hold of you—" He broke off as he caught sight of something across the room and then continued softly, "Hullo! What's this? A *toy* cupboard! The very hidey-hole, I'll swear!"

The little people blinked as daylight flooded in suddenly through the windows of the dolls' house. Harwell Mincing had flung open the toy-cupboard doors.

"Damnation take the creatures! They are in here somewhere!" he stormed, as he rifled through the jumble of toys on the upper shelves at his eye-level.

Finding nothing, he stepped back. Then, for the first time, he caught sight of the dolls' house tucked away at the bottom of the cupboard.

"Of course! Where else?" he cried, triumphantly. "Where better to conceal doll-size manikins than in a dolls' establishment!"

Harwell stooped, picked up the dolls' house and carried it across to the nursery table.

Spelbush, Brelca and Fistram dived for cover behind the furniture as Harwell's eye peered in at a downstairs window.

"I know you're in there! Believe me, little ones, I haven't pursued you these long months not to know when I'm close to holding you in my hands at last!"

His fingers shook with excitement as he fumbled with the catch that opened the front of the dolls' house. After all this time! After all those infuriating failures and near-misses! But all that was behind him now, he told himself. Success was his at last—and with it riches and a life of luxury from now on!

The catch came free on the side of the dolls' house and, at his touch, the entire front wall swung open. The Lilliputians cowered in their separate hiding places as Harwell's gloating face stared in.

"Come now, my children, this is no time to hide your pretty faces!" he said teasingly. Now that the little creatures were finally his, he was happy to savour the precious moments of victory. "The game is over and I've won!" he crooned. "We're going to be friends, my little ones. There's no sense in hiding from me any longer. I shall exhibit you in front of every crowned head in Europe. We shall cross the vast American continent together. I shall make you famous, little creatures, while you, in turn, shall make me rich!"

Then, unable to contain himself a moment longer, he reached a trembling hand inside to shift the furniture behind which the Lilliputians were concealed.

"Come out, come out—wherever you are!" he said with an evil chuckle.

135

"It's the master's 'ouse what's up for sale, sir," said a voice behind him. "It ain't the one what the dollies lives in."

Harwell swung round, surprised at having been caught prying, to discover Millie standing in the nursery doorway. She was carrying a coal scuttle and had come upstairs to stoke the nursery fire.

"I . . . I came in to inspect the—er—nursery," mumbled Harwell. "I—er—could not help but admire the fine wee dolls' hoose."

"I know," said Millie, understandingly, crossing the room and kneeling on the rug by the fireplace. She could appreciate how the missionary had felt drawn to the dolls' house. She had the self-same admiration for it herself. "It ain't 'arf a real right corker of a dollies 'ouse, ain't it?" she said.

"Aye, aye—it is indeed!" said Harwell, wishing that the housemaid would get on with her business, put some coal on the fire and clear off. As he spoke, he kept one hand behind his back, his long fingers cautiously exploring the inside of the dolls' house.

"It belongs to Miss Philippa, sir," said Millie, chattily. "Leastways, it's supposed to do—you wouldn't 'ardly think so though, not if you knew 'ow much time Master Gerald spends, sitting at that very table, playing at dollies 'ouses with 'is sister."

"Is that a fact—the noo?" said Harwell, coldly, his fingers still feeling around the dolls' house floor.

The Lilliputians inside had no difficulty at all in dodging Harwell's probing fingers while his back was turned to them.

Spelbush tiptoed around the walls of the room towards

the front of the dolls' house. He motioned to Brelca and Fistram to accompany him. Harwell Mincing's roaming fingers inside the ground-floor rooms had given Spelbush an idea.

"Still—it's nice, ain't it, when brothers and sisters gets on together an' no fallings out," said Millie, shovelling coal on to the red embers in the grate. "Leastways," she added, "that's what I allus says."

"Do you not have chores to do aboot the hoose, lassie?" said Harwell, wishing that the housemaid would leave him alone in the room. "Does it not pain your employer that you spend so much time in idle gossip?"

During all this, the little people had crept out, unnoticed, on to the nursery table and were now taking a firm grip on the open hinged front wall of the dolls' house.

"Lor', sir!" said Millie. "Why, Mr Garstanton don't mind gossip, sir! As for *pain*, sir—a little bit of chit-chat never 'urt nobody, did it now?"

But Millie was never to learn whether or not the visitor agreed or disagreed with her views on "chit-chat" and whether it might or might not cause a person pain. She had barely got the words out of her mouth when Harwell, it seemed, was in terrible pain himself.

"Yeeooo*OW*!" he screamed, and leapt a foot in the air.

While Millie had been speaking, the little people, having taken their firm hold on the front of the dolls' house, had tugged hard, and slammed it shut on Harwell's fingers.

Harwell shook his hand in the air, blew on it, sucked the ends of his fingers and then shook them in the air again.

"Are you all right, sir?" said Millie, puzzled.

"Oooh! Aaahhh! *Ow!*" replied Harwell. "Quite all right,

thank you," he moaned. "Just a touch of pins-and-needles, that's all."

"Pins-and-needles, sir? Do you get them as well?" said Millie, sympathetically. "I'm a reg'lar martyr to 'em!"

As Millie spoke, she got to her feet. The Lilliputians meanwhile had been making their way, unseen, from the nursery table to the floor by scrambling down a chair.

"It's in my toes where I gets it most," continued Millie. "Night-times like as not—which is what comes from lying in a cold bed, as my old mum allus used to reckon. I 'as to get up then, and sit on the edge of the bed and wiggle 'em. 'Ere! 'Appen you should try wiggling your fingers, eh?"

"I'm perfectly all right now, girl," snapped Harwell, as the cruel pain ebbed to a throbbing ache. "I'll thank ye to get aboot your business now and leave me to mine."

"Very good, sir," said Millie, as it became plain that her presence was not wanted. She moved to lift the dolls' house from the nursery table. "I'll just move this out of your way," she said.

"Hands off that, miss!" said Harwell, sharply, moving between the housemaid and the dolls' house.

"But it don't belong on that table, sir. I've told them two scallywags time and time again! 'Put your toys away,' I says, 'when you've finished with 'em. They ain't to be left on the nursery table,' I says, 'not when I 'as to lay up for nursery tea.' "

Now the Lilliputians had crept out from under the table and were taking the attack into their enemy's camp. They had managed to untie his bootlaces and had then knotted the lace of his left boot to that of his right.

"Leave the dolls' house where it is, girl," said Harwell, waving an impatient hand at Millie.

"If you says so, sir," said Millie, doubtfully.

The Lilliputians, meanwhile, having completed their task, had shot away and were now hiding behind a footstool.

"I do say so, girl!" snapped Harwell. "And I'd be grateful now to be left undisturbed—your master has agreed that I'm to be granted total privacy."

"Well, sir," said Millie picking up the coal scuttle and heading for the door, "if you're quite sure there ain't nothing I can do . . ."

"Nothing! Nothing! Leave me to myself! Do you consider me incapable of standing on my own two feet? YeeaaAAGH!"

Harwell's second anguished cry was uttered as he appeared to answer his own question.

No, he was *not*, it seemed, capable of standing on his own two feet.

He had just tried to take a step across the room and his knotted bootlaces had brought him crashing down, full length, on the nursery floor.

The Lilliputians, peeping over the top of the footstool, had difficulty in holding back their laughter.

Millie went and knelt by Harwell's side. "Mercy me, sir!" she said in some concern. "You did come down a pearler an' no mistake! 'Ave you 'urt yourself?"

Harwell sat up, scowled, dusted himself down and felt for broken bones. "Leave me alone, girl," he growled, pulling himself to a sitting position. "I'm perfectly well—I must have tripped or something."

"You probably fell over one of the kiddies' toys, I expects," said Millie. "What did I say, not two minutes since, about them leaving their playthings out where folks can trip—" Millie broke off in some surprise as she caught sight of Harwell's feet. "No, it worn't a toy at all, sir—beggin' y'r pardin—it's your lices!"

"My lices?" echoed Harwell, not understanding the housemaid's cockney accent and wondering what on earth she was babbling on about now.

"Your *boot*-lices, sir. You've got 'em tied together. Whatever was you thinking of to go and do a funny thing like that?"

Harwell realized with horror what had happened. The cunning creatures had got down, somehow, out of the dolls' house and were roaming around the floor. If he didn't make a move to capture them soon they would be gone from the room and heading beyond his reach.

"Come along, girl—out!" he cried, reaching down and snapping the knot that held his boots together.

"If you're sure you ain't done yourself any grievous harm," said Millie, still concerned. To tell the truth, she was rather worried about leaving the visitor alone in the room. A man who ties his own laces together might be capable of—well—anything! "That was a real right corker you came down," she added.

"Out! Out! Out!" stormed Harwell, scrambling to his feet and bustling Millie towards the landing. "I have work to do, and I insist on doing it in private."

As Harwell propelled Millie through the door, Spelbush beckoned again to his companions.

"Here! Give me a hand," he said.

Another battle-plan had occurred to the leader of the trio of little people.

Spelbush led his troops across to the children's bagatelle board which was propped up against the wall. With

Fistram's help, he pushed open the compartment where the steel balls were stored.

Snatching up the first ball, Spelbush weighed it carefully in his hand, took aim, then bowled it across the nursery carpet.

The bagatelle ball sped swiftly, silently and smoothly across the floor and out on to the landing. It came to a rest only inches away from Harwell's feet.

"And this time, remember, I am not to be disturbed on any account!" Harwell called over the banister-rail to Millie who was on her way downstairs.

"Very good, sir!"

Meanwhile, unknown to Harwell, more bagatelle balls were rolling out of the nursery and coming to a stop close to his boots.

It was a joint effort on the part of the Lilliputians. Fistram was lifting the balls out of the bagatelle board and passing them to Brelca who, in turn, handed them on to Spelbush.

Harwell, unaware of the steel balls dotted all around his feet, smiled to himself craftily as he watched Millie disappear around the well in the staircase.

"And now, my cunning little creatures," he muttered softly to himself, "you and I have several scores to settle— Yeeeaa*aAAAGGGHHH*!"

This third, and by far the loudest, cry of anguish and surprise was bellowed by Harwell as he stepped on several of the steel balls all at once and his feet shot out from under him. He fell, backwards and head-over-heels, down the flight of stairs.

Harwell, having performed several rather clumsy somersaults on the way, tumbled on to the first-floor landing. He arrived at exactly the same time as Millie, despite the fact that she had set off some twenty seconds before him. He lay in a crumpled moaning heap, aching from head to foot.

"Oooh, sir," said Millie, looking down at Harwell, "it ain't been your lucky day at all, sir—'as it?"

Harwell's fall down the stairs, accompanied by his cries of pain *en route*, had caused doors to be flung open all over the house.

"What's all the racket up there?" cried Mr Garstanton from the door of his studio.

"Fair gave me a start, it did!" cried Cook, standing at the kitchen door.

And the door of the parlour, too, had opened and a black-veiled figure was now standing on the first-floor landing gazing down, sourly, at the whimpering Harwell.

"Get up, you weak, incompetent fool!" hissed Sarah.

"Give me your hand, sister," begged Harwell.

"My hand? My hand!" screeched Sarah. "If you were burning in the eternal fire of damnation, brother, I would not stretch out my little finger to save you!"

With which, tightlipped, she swept past Harwell down the stairs, passing on her way both Cook and Mr Garstanton going up to see what all the commotion was about.

They heard the front door slam behind Sarah.

Philippa and Gerald had also come out of the parlour and were standing over Harwell. His false ginger beard had come adrift in the fall and was hanging off his face.

"It's him again!" hissed Philippa at her brother.

"I know!" Gerald whispered back.

Gerald pointed to the upper landing where, just beyond the banister-rail, three tiny figures were dancing with glee.

" 'E didn't 'arf come a cropper, sir," said Millie to Mr

Garstanton who had now arrived outside the parlour. " 'E fair *bounced* down each and every single one o' them stairs."

Harwell glanced around, wildly, at the faces peering down at him.

He had had his fingers trapped in the dolls' house wall. He had been brought down full-length on the nursery floor. He had had his feet taken from under him on the landing and he had tumbled down two flights of stairs. His beard hung off his face. His wig had been pushed down over one eye. He was black and blue all over.

He had had enough. His only wish was to get out of the Garstanton house.

Harwell scrambled to his feet, clutching at his beard with one hand and pushing at his wig with the other. "Good-day to you, sir," he bleated at Mr Garstanton as he moved to pass him.

"Do I take it, reverend, that you won't be buying the house?" enquired the photographer, still puzzled as to what was going on.

"Buying it?" gabbled Harwell. "Buying it! I would not buy this hell-hole, sir, if it came free, gratis, and with a king's ransom thrown in for good measure!"

With which, he pulled off the loose beard, stuffed it into Mr Garstanton's hands and fled down the stairs.

The front door slammed behind him.

"Well I never!" said Mr Garstanton.

"Nice manners, I must say, for a religious gentleman," said Cook.

"Some folks is full of themselves," said Millie.

"We mustn't rush to make judgements on the poor fellow," said Mr Garstanton, turning the false beard over in his hands still without any idea as to what it all meant.

"Africa can do strange things to people—the heat, you know. Pity about the house, though. Never mind. I'm sure we will sell it soon. Perhaps that nice family from Middlesborough who came to look at it last week will give us a favourable decision."

The children exchanged a secret smile.

Up on the top landing the Lilliputians shook hands and did a little jig. Despite their lack of height, they had managed to get the better of the Mincings yet again.

EPILOGUE

The "FOR SALE" sign outside the Garstanton house had gone. In its place stood another sign that said "SOLD".

A large removal van, pulled by two white shire horses, stood outside the house. The rear doors of the van were open and inside was most of the Garstantons' furniture. Next to the van, there was a horse-drawn cab parked in the street. Sitting inside the cab were Millie and Cook both clutching carpet bags which contained their most prized personal belongings.

"I can't think what's keeping the master and the children," said Millie.

"We'll miss that train if they don't come soon," said Cook.

Two removal men, in green baize aprons, carried a horsehair sofa out of the house and loaded it into the back of the removal van.

"I think that's the lot," said the first removal man. "But we'd better make a final check."

Mr Garstanton, standing in the hall, glanced absent-mindedly at the spot where the grandfather clock had always stood. But the big clock, like everything else, had been put inside the van. He took his watch out of his waistcoat pocket instead and flicked it open with his thumb-nail.

"On parade, the Brigade of Guards!" he called up the stairs.

"Shan't be a minute, Grandfather!" Gerald's voice floated down from the nursery.

"We're just saying 'goodbye' to the nursery," called Philippa.

"Sharp's the word then!" shouted Mr Garstanton. Then, turning to the two removal men who had just come in again, he said, "You will check that nothing's left upstairs, won't you?"

"I've been in this business over twenty years, guv'nor," said the first removal man, touching his forehead with his forefinger, "and I've never been known to slip up yet." And, turning to his companion, he said, "Have a last look round up above."

The second removal man nodded in reply and set off up the stairs.

Gerald and Philippa, wearing their outdoor things, were sitting on the bare boards of the nursery floor. They were talking to their little friends, the Lilliputians, who were standing on the ground floor of the dolls' house.

Everything else from the nursery had gone into the removal van. The toy cupboard, a built-in fixture, stood empty. Even the dolls' house furniture had been put into a packing case with the other toys.

"Are you *sure* you want to travel to the country in the dolls' house?" said Gerald to the little people. "Wouldn't you rather come with us on the train?"

"I could easily smuggle you into Millie's carpet bag," said Philippa.

"No, thank you, little girl," said Brelca.

"You first brought us to this house, you may recall,

inside Millie's carpet bag," said Spelbush, stiffly.

"And that was after a long train journey too," said Fistram.

It seemed a long, long time ago now, but it was true. The children had been on holiday, the summer before, when they had found the shipwrecked Lilliputians on the beach. They had brought the little people back to their home in the city.

"It wasn't a very comfortable train ride," said Brelca. "My clothes got *very* creased."

"We didn't get anything to eat for *hours*," said Fistram.

"And, what is more, it wasn't very dignified," said Spelbush. "We shall travel to the country inside this dolls' house inside the removal van."

Gerald and Philippa looked at each other, doubtfully.

"Gerald! Philippa! You must come down at once!" called their grandfather from the hall below.

"Coming!" Gerald called back.

"See you in the country then," said Philippa to the little people as she closed the front of the dolls' house on them.

"Have a pleasant journey," said Gerald, as he dropped the catch on the dolls' house wall.

"See you in the country!" cried the little people from inside the dolls' house.

The children got to their feet, crossed to the door and turned for a last look at the nursery. It looked so much bigger with all the toys and furniture gone—only the dolls' house left standing in the middle of the empty floor.

As the children moved across the landing, they saw the second removal man who had come up from down below.

"You won't forget to carry the dolls' house down, will you?" said Gerald.

"You will be careful with it, won't you?" said Philippa, anxiously.

"Leave it to me, young master and young missie," said the second removal man. "I'll see it's well taken care of!"

The children scampered down the stairs, much relieved.

The second removal man went into the nursery and stood looking down at the dolls' house.

A smile spread slowly across his face.

He rubbed his hands together.

"He who laughs last, laughs longest," said Harwell Mincing with an evil chuckle.

He had managed to get himself a job as a temporary removal man on the very day, he knew, that the children were moving to the country.

"Is there anything left up there?" called the first removal man from the floor below.

"Only a dolls' house!" Harwell shouted back. "I'll bring it down!"

He picked up the dolls' house gently, mindful of its precious contents. He knew the cunning creatures were inside. He had stood on the landing outside and heard the Garstanton brats talking to the little manikins. He was not now going to let the dolls' house out of his sight. When the time was ripe, he would make off with it. There was no hurry. For the rest of the morning, at least, he would go on with the pretence of being a removal man.

That very afternoon, he would be a millionaire!

Still laughing quietly to himself, he set off down the stairs carrying the dolls' house and its priceless living cargo.

"Off we go at last then," said Mr Garstanton, slamming the

door of the cab and beaming all around at Gerald, Philippa, Millie and Cook.

"I say, eh?" said Cook. "Off to the country!"

"What excitement!" said Millie. "I'm even looking forward to it now—all that there countryside—it'll be like another world!"

The children too were excited at the prospect of an entirely different way of life.

"Drive on, cabbie!" said Mr Garstanton.

The driver flicked his whip and the horse and cab set off at a rattle along the cobbled street.

Harwell watched the cab move away as he lifted the dolls' house up on to the driving-seat of the removal van.

"Do we have to have that up here," said the first removal man, grumpily. "Won't it go in the back with everything else?"

"It wouldn't do for it to be tossed around," replied Harwell with a shake of his head. "There are valuable things inside."

Harwell clambered up on to the seat next to his work-mate, picked up the dolls' house and rested it on his lap.

"Gee-up, there!" said the first removal man, flicking the reins of the two shire horses.

As the removal van lumbered off along the street, Harwell hugged the dolls' house to his chest and chuckled softly yet again.

"What's amusing you?" said the first removal man.

"Nothing—nothing," said Harwell innocently, keeping his precious secret to himself.

He would not have been quite so pleased with life, though, had he noticed that one of the rear windows of the dolls' house was open wide.

But he would find out soon enough that the dolls' house was quite empty—the Lilliputians had already gone.

Inside the nursery, the creak of the toy-cupboard door echoed noisily through the empty house.

Spelbush, Fistram and Brelca, who had all three slipped out through the dolls' house rear window when Harwell had entered the room, came out of the toy cupboard slowly, one by one.

They gazed around at the bare walls of the nursery. The room seemed so much bigger now that there was nothing in it.

"I, Spelbush Frelock, navigator and explorer," began Spelbush, holding up his sword-hilt in front of his face, "do claim this uninhabited dwelling-place and situate garden territories in the name of his most mighty maj—"

"Oh, do shut up, Spelbush," said Brelca and Fistram together.

"What's the matter now?" asked Spelbush.

"Every solitary stitch of clothing that I possess went off in that removal van," said Brelca.

"The cook's gone off to the country," said Fistram, sorrowfully. "There'll be no more pink blancmange."

"A plumstone for all the pink blancmanges in the world, Fistram," snapped Spelbush. "And another plumstone, Brelca, for all your vanished clothing." He waved his sword at the nursery window. "There is a world out there, waiting to be conquered!"

"I shall miss those children," said Brelca, sadly.

"Me too," sniffed Fistram.

"I shall miss them as well," said Spelbush. "But it had to happen sooner or later. We couldn't depend on them to feed and clothe us for ever. We have to learn to stand on our own two feet. We must go out and explore this country and meet adventure as it comes."

"I've had enough of exploration," said Brelca.

"I've had *more* than enough adventures to last me a lifetime," said Fistram.

"Plumstones to the pair of you! Why—the explorations and adventurings have only just begun!" cried Spelbush, bravely.

Brelca and Fistram exchanged a glance. Perhaps Spelbush was right. After all, they had sailed across eight oceans in order to get here—they couldn't spend all their time just sitting around in a nursery. Perhaps it *was* time that they did some conquering . . .

Spelbush, his sword held at the ready and with his two companions at his side, set off across the bare boards of the nursery floor towards the wide and wonderful giants' world that lay beyond.